FERNDALE
ASSIGNMENT

Dan Smeenge

Dan Smeenge

Copyright 2018 ©Dan Smeenge
ISBN-13: 978-1-7327997-2-1
ISBN-10: 1-7327997-2-5

DEDICATION

I dedicate this book to my wife,
who believes in me.

Dan Smeenge

TABLE OF CONTENTS

Dan Smeenge

CHAPTER ONE

Russell pulled on to the highway and thought what a silly thing he was doing. He had loaded his possessions in the back of his car and closed up the rental apartment. Now he was heading to another state to a house he bought, sight unseen. His realtor, an old friend of his, said it was a good deal. The land itself was worth the price he paid and there were a house and a barn as well. Still, he had an uneasy feeling.

Maybe it was just because Russell had never bought anything major before. Maybe it was because he had just retired. Maybe it was because his mother had just died and he had all that grief to deal with. Really, he should not have made such a big jump at this time in his life.

But Russell was used to challenges, to new things, to new cultures, new languages, even new countries. He had served as a missionary for almost thirty years, but he had never been so trepidatious of any new place as he was of Ferndale.

The house was on a well treed three acres lot. What used to be a highway was along one side. The images on the advertisement were fuzzy so Russell looked it up on the internet. The satellite picture showed the house and barn alright, and a nice front yard with some sort of a colorful blur that could be a bush or lawn ornament. The information indicated that the house had been used as a small hotel or guesthouse when traffic went by on the old road. But they had built a new highway that bypassed Ferndale. The former owners died or moved away so his dealings were with the nephew, as he understood it. The man was all too happy to accept his low offer.

It was just over a two hours drive from where Russell had lived near Chicago. Close enough to get to the airport, yet far enough away to be in a rural part of Michigan. His main concern was how he was going to fill his days. Perhaps there would be enough work fixing the house to keep his mind off the fact that he was living in America.

It was Russell's mother's sudden illness and death that brought him home. He had been on his way to a new assignment, but after he was home and had dealt with his mother's estate he decided it was time to retire. Well, it was a joint decision. Funding for missions was way down and the agency encouraged him to see this as a new season.

Russell decided to invest the funds from his mother's estate in property. He pulled off the main road and drove through the small town that was to be his new home. There were a few people on the street. From the diversity of ethnicities and dusty pickups, he concluded that this was a hot spot for migrant workers.

It didn't take Russell long to find the old highway. According to the map, his house was right along here someplace. He found the old mailbox, leaning almost to the ground. Stopping and checking the numbers he discovered he was home. Well, that's job number one, he thought to himself, as he admired how the mailbox was almost unusable. He pulled up the long dirt driveway and saw his house for the first time.

The key was to be under the mat, but Russell noticed that there was a light on in the kitchen. That may be to scare away burglars, he thought. It was quite a large place, maybe eight or nine rooms for guests. He was surprised that it looks so nice. The advertisement hadn't done it justice. He was surprised at the nice porch wrapping around two sides. He was surprised that the kitchen door was open, but mostly he was surprised that the lady in the kitchen had a shotgun pointed at him.

"Go away," she said in a heavy accent. "Get off my property!" she added.

It took Russell a few seconds to catch his breath and get his wits about him. He tried to explain that he had just bought the house. He stammered that it was actually his, but it's hard to argue with a grand motherly looking lady with a shotgun.

He glanced around the room, searching for a clue for how to peacefully end this situation. He'd had guns pointed at him before, but never by a little old grandmother. Although it was a warm day, she was wearing a wool sweater, "Definitely homemade," he thought. Her mix of other layers was so totally mismatched it looked like her wardrobe was having an argument. He saw dried leaves hanging from a nail on the wall. "Looks like mountain sage." He said to himself.

He noticed the Turkish coffee pot and the double stacking teapot on the otherwise empty counter. Then his eyes fell on two triangular blocks of wood hanging from a string. They were about five inches along each side with one concave side. Something clicked in his mind, switching quickly to a language he once knew. He asked in his best Albanian for a cup of tea.

The request surprised her. She put her gun down and promptly made tea. Obviously, the drive to be courteous to guests was greater than the drive to shoot them.

Over the cup of tea, Russell discovered that it was her husband that had started the guesthouse. After he died she tried to carry on, but her husband had given power of attorney to his brother's son who lived in New York. And for years this nephew had tried to get her to move out, and to sell the place.

This was her home and had been for almost forty-five years. She was not going to move. Everything she had left her country for was here. All her memories were here. Where would she go? She was too old and too scared to travel.

"There is no way that they can make me move." she said, "So, I don't care if you own my house, it's still mine."

Russell was quiet for a few minutes, absorbing all the new information, then a solution became very clear.

"Who says you have to move?" he asked. "There is plenty of room for the two of us here. There's lots of work for me to do. Maybe we can open up the guesthouse again. I'm quite a good handyman."

"Yes, that's what this place needs," she said, "a handyman. You can be my handyman."

So from that point on Liria Shihini referred to him as the handyman. She maintained the role of the owner of the house no matter what the deed said and who paid the bills.

As Russell went back to his car to get his bags, he realized he had just met the colorful blur on the front yard.

After he came back in he was given a brief tour of the house. Upstairs it smelled musty like no one had opened a window for years. Being as tired as he was he did not remember much. He chose a room as sensibly far away from Liria's as was polite. He was not sure he could trust her, and from the way he was being watched, the feeling was mutual.

He was about to get ready for bed when Liria knocked on his door.

"If you want some supper, it is ready now," she said.

In all the excitement Russell had forgotten about food. Supper was a pastry made with feta cheese, served alongside rice with beans. The primary flavor in both dishes was olive oil. Not the expensive kind, but the stuff that came in a gallon tin can. It had first been used to fry meat or fish then carefully saved to add to other dishes. As his taste buds remembered the flavors his mind remembered where he was. Ferndale probably did not have an international grocery store. This meant that the pastry and cheese were likely homemade.

The dinner conversation was mostly one-sided. It was Liria's mental list of things that needed to be fixed around the place. It was obvious to Russell that she considered his job as handyman already started.

Although Russell wished to sleep in the next day, this proved true the next morning. Liria woke him up at six o'clock with a call to breakfast. They were going to have to come to some sort of agreement about time, he thought. Over breakfast she was quiet, just looking at him, trying to figure him out.

"How did you know, I was from Albania," she asked finally.

"I lived there for almost a year during the Kosovan war." He paused, remembering that time. "It was mostly your dress, the mountain sage hanging on the wall and the teapot and coffeepot. They gave me clues. But when I saw those wooden blocks I was quite convinced. I had seen them before being worn by village women that come into town. I don't know of any other culture, where the women wear blocks like that on their hips."

"Yes, those were my mother's. She gave them to me on my wedding day. Just a week or two before we came to America," she said, slowly remembering her mother, her wedding and that trip with every word.

"I have not worn them here, but I keep them as a reminder of where I come from."

The talk went a little easier then. They introduced themselves realizing that they had forgotten to do so earlier. They tried to figure out who was going to buy the food and who was going to cook; who was going too clean what and when, and who was to pay what bill. In the end, no matter what they agreed on, he paid everything and she cleaned and cooked.

He also insisted that she called him "Russell" but she always called him "Mr. Green".

CHAPTER TWO

It took the first two weeks to get things settled out. There was the toilet to fix, outlets to replace, windows to get moving again and a list of other things that just needed cleaning and patching up. It was when he called the phone company to order Internet that he found out the phone bill had not been paid for two months. Deciding that it would be better face to face, Russell drove into town to transfer the phone into his name as well as the other utilities for the house.

It was quite an informative day. Not only had the phone bill not been paid, the lights, water and gas were delinquent as well.

It seemed that all the bills had been paid by the nephew up until a few months ago. Probably in an attempt to get Liria to move out, he stopped paying them. The utility companies assumed the check was in the mail and kept Liria connected. But now these were all his responsibility. This raised questions in Russell's mind.

"How have you been living here? I mean what do you do for money?" he asked Liria over a cup of tea.

"I had some money saved." was all she said.

"Well, do you get any income from Social Security?"

"What's that?"

Deciding a different tactic, Russell asked, "Did your husband pay all the bills?"

"Yes, too many bills, government bills, insurance bills, electric bills, all bills, bills, bills!"

"Well, one of those bills had to have been Social Security. When he died they would pay you money, every month. Do you get this money?" he asked cautiously.

"Why would somebody pay me just because my husband died?" she asked.

"Because it's money you've earned and have put away to take out later."

"Somebody is going to pay me money because somebody died?" she asked questioningly. "Maybe if enough people die, I will be rich?"

"No, Social Security is money that your husband put into a safe place for you to get after he died," he explained slowly.

"Yes, he did that, I'll show you," Liria said as she got up off her chair and went to the kitchen sink. She pulled back the rug in front of the sink and pulled up some loose floorboards.

"See, this is where he kept the money for me, but it is all gone now."

This was going to be harder than he thought. He was used to conveying ideas in different cultures, but he hadn't expected this in Ferndale.

"Social Security is money the government has set aside for you. Did you ever send in papers to the government after your husband died?" he asked hopefully.

"Why would the government want to know when my husband died?"

He thought better than to try and answer this question. Changing directions again, he asked, "Do you have a coroner's report? A death certificate?"

"What is that?"

"When somebody dies, a man comes out and signs a paper saying that he is dead. Did this happen when your husband died?"

"Why would I need somebody to tell me my husband is dead? I know what dead looks like."

"You would need the paper to get him buried in a cemetery. Then you use that paper to get his insurance money and your Social Security money." He was clearly using terms she had never heard of before.

"Oh, there is no problem then, because he is not buried in a cemetery," she answered with a smile.

"Then where is he buried?" Russell asked cautiously.

"By that tree over there." Liria pointed to the backyard as she got up to put away the teacups.

By this time Russell's head was in his hands, elbows resting on the table. "Did anybody help you?" He was afraid of the answer.

"I did not need help. I was stronger then. I could dig a hole. I used the wheelbarrow to get him over there."

Russell did not want to push it any further. Liria, thinking that everything was settled, went on with the dishes. Russell poured himself another cup of tea and went up to his room. This was going to be more work than fixing up the old house. He realized what was going to have to happen.

After Russell had thought things through he picked up the phone and called the police station. He thought he better start at the top and asked to speak to the chief of police. After a brief explanation of what he was calling about, the chief decided he had better come out and talk personally with Liria and himself.

About five minutes later, Russell was surprised to see a '59 Edsel pull into his yard. A man in a polo shirt and casual slacks got out. He looked to be in his mid-fifties. Russell went out to greet him.

"Thanks for coming, I'm Russell Green," he said as he shook the officer's hand.

"Dave May, just call me Dave," said the Chief of Police.

"Is this what they use for cop cars these days?" Russell asked as he looked at the Edsel.

"It's my personal car," said Dave, "It's just as good as a real cop car because everybody knows that it's mine." Dave leaned against the side of the enormous hood and folded his arms. "Why don't we just have a chat out here before I talk to Liria?"

For the next half hour, Russell filled him in on who he was and when and why he bought the place. The events of his first meeting with Liria made Dave laugh.

"There has been no real crime committed, so don't worry about that. Since you own the place outright, by filling in a few forms, Mr. Shihini can stay resting peacefully where he is." Dave said thoughtfully, still turning the facts over in his head.

"But if he has paid for life insurance and Social Security, Liria has a lot of money coming to her if we can prove that he's dead."

"I'd rather let sleeping dogs lie, pardon the expression," Dave said, starting to walk over to the tree in the backyard. "But if you're right, and there's money coming to her, we might have to dig him up."

"I'd hate to do that, I don't even know how long he's been dead. Can't we just take her word for it?" Russell asked.

"I'd like to, but personally I would not take Liria's word for anything," Dave said with a smile. "Besides, the trouble is that all the agencies are going to need a regular certificate. That needs to be signed, and it can't get signed unless it's been witnessed. And it can't get witnessed unless we have visual proof." Dave finished gravely.

They walked in through the back door of the house and found Liria still in the kitchen.

"Good afternoon, Liria," said Dave.

"Good afternoon Officer May," Liria returned.

"I hear you might have some money coming to you, if what Russell here says is true. Would you mind if he looked through some of your husband's paperwork? We're looking for some very specific papers that we would recognize when we saw them."

"Sure, if you promise not to mess anything up. They're all on his desk," she said as she got up and opened the door off the kitchen. It led into what looked like had once been a pantry, but was evidently Mr. Shihini's office.

A small table was piled high with shoe boxes and loose stacks of papers and envelopes. A tornado could not mess up the stacks any worse. It was obvious that nobody had been in here since the late Mr. Shihini left it, who knows how many years ago. There was even evidence of a half-drunk cup of coffee that had long ago evaporated. An ashtray, overflowing with cigarette butts was the central object on the table.

Russell said he would get right on it, but wanted to see the officer to his car. The two men left the house by the front door.

"I think I have the easy job. I just have to dig up a dead body and prove he is who he was. I'd rather do that than dig through the pile on that table. Who knows what you are going to run into," said Dave. "Give me a call if you find anything," he added handing Russell a business card with his number on it. "And by the way, welcome to the neighborhood. Glad you are here."

Russell watched Dave drive out in the yard and stood there for a few minutes with his hands in his pockets. Just a few weeks ago, he was driving to this place and wondering if he would find enough to do to fill his days. The mountain of paperwork ahead of him would keep him busy for quite some time.

He knew he would need some sort of box to start filing things in. He rummaged through the house and found some old milk crates and other cardboard boxes that would do. But as he would need some files, he took a trip into town. At the general store, he stocked up on files and hanging folders, pens and labels, and anything else he thought he would need. He also noticed he was low on gas so he pulled into the discount station and filled up. He handed the man behind the window his money and with his change the clerk asked, "So when are they going to dig him up?"

'Evidently, news travels fast in this small town,' he thought.

That evening Russell made headway by just throwing away things that were obviously trash. The ashtray was the first thing to go. Soon he was able to get the window open and let fresh air into the room. The breeze that blew in was scented with pine. He was thankful that it soon replaced that stale cigarette smell around him. But it didn't take long to run out of steam. He needed some inspiration. Music would help. He got out his small MP3 player and speakers. Years ago his nephew had helped him transfer all his music from cassette tapes to CDs. Then just recently he had moved it all onto the small MP3 player he received as a Christmas present. He took his time trying to find just the right music for the job, and when he found it, he smiled, tapped the play button and the music of Bela Fleck and the Flecktones filled the office.

On the second day, he found the insurance papers. On the third, he found the tax records. Tody Shihini was a US citizen and had paid taxes. 'Good,' thought Russell, 'it's a start.'

Regularly throughout the day, Liria kept them supplied with fresh tea or coffee. Her frequent visits to the ever-changing office never revealed whether she was pleased or sad at the change. Russell kept plodding on. He put photographs that he found in an album. Addresses and letters were placed in a separate box. Stacks of empty cigarette packs were thrown out, along with countless dried-up pens and pencils stubs. He carefully cleaned objects that might have sentimental value. These were placed on the newly dusted shelves. The carcass of a long-dead mouse was unceremoniously disposed of.

Daily he was at the town hall, filing papers, finding copies of deeds, even doing some research in the local library. He also found a good reason to be in town over lunch. Liria was in the habit of making enough of one dish to make it last a week, so if he wanted any variety in his diet he had to eat lunch out.

He ran into Dave on the fourth day of sorting.

"Found any more bodies?" joked Dave.

"Just a mouse. Do you want to exhume him too while you're at it?" replied Russell.

"Only if he had an insurance policy," said Dave. "Speaking of, did you find anything?"

"Yes, he had it all. Social Security, insurance, even the title to a '64 Ford pickup. So all we need now is the certificate. Guess you better come out and dig him up."

"I'll need Liria's permission. If you let her know, I'll bring the papers when we come. How does Monday sound?"

"I'll let her know." Said Russell, "but how will we know it's really him?"

"I have been checking into that because he probably won't look quite himself. I did find out that he went to a dentist once. We have those records, so we'll go with that."

"By the way," added Dave, "check the barn for that pick-up."

Upon that, Russell realized he had been so busy at the house, he never once looked in the barn.

That evening he sat Liria down at the office table and went over all that he had found. First, he showed her the picture album and waited while she explained who each and every person was. It was then that he learned she had a younger sister. She was probably still living in Albania. Her parents had died years ago.

Russell showed her the souvenirs he had found from Chicago and Detroit and she explained how they had taken two vacations in their life and had collected these things. She had forgotten where they were. Watching her looking at them, he wondered if she was reliving the few fun days she'd had in her life. Then he got to the paperwork.

Liria was surprised to learn how much she would be getting every month from Social Security. Although small in comparison to most people, to her it was a fortune.

"And there's a life insurance policy. All we have to do is provide them with a death certificate and you get the money." Russell was trying to choose his words carefully.

"How much more money?" Asked Liria.

He paused, then answered, "One hundred thousand dollars."

She almost passed out.

"When do I get the money?" she asked breathlessly.

"When we can prove that your husband died."

"How do we do that?"

"We have to dig him up."

She jumped out of her chair and headed toward the door.

"Wait, where are you going?" asked Russell.

"To get some shovels!"

It took some time to convince her that they could not do it that way. He explained that a team would be coming out on Monday with a backhoe and papers to sign. He underlined that an official from the government had to be there, but that she did not if it would be too hard on her to see the body of her husband.

"You only have to give them your permission, okay?"

"Give them my permission? Yes, and I'll give them a cake too!"

True to her word, when the men came on Monday, the kitchen table was layered with cakes, cookies and other Albanian delicacies. There were fresh coffee and tea and a large pitcher of lemonade.

A few hours later, a positive identification had been made, and the certificate signed that yes, Tody Shihini was dead. The body was placed in a plain wooden coffin inside a concrete vault placed at the bottom of the now official gravesite.

Liria's sunny disposition changed when she realized that these men did not bring her hundred thousand with them. Not only that but she would have to pay for the coffin and the vault. But that payment could wait until the insurance money came in.

Monday night they celebrated with steaks cooked on the grill, with baked potatoes and greens picked from the garden. Russell breathed deep, noticing that the American barbecue had an aroma all of its own.

"Liria, just how long ago did your husband die?" asked Russell.

"Let's see, must be two years now, yes, just over two years," answered Liria.

"How have you gotten along, I mean how did you pay for groceries or bills for those two years?"

"I never saw any bills, I think the nephew paid them. But every Monday I would go to the place under the floor and take out fifty dollars for my groceries and other needs," she said.

He did some mental math and figured out that there had been over five thousand in cash under the floorboards.

"Didn't you have a bank account?" he asked.

"Tody did not believe in banks."

"You will probably need one now. One hundred thousand dollars should not be kept in the floorboards of the kitchen. Don't worry, I'll help you set up an account and show you how to use it." Saying this made him realize how much more work there was to do before this matter was settled.

CHAPTER THREE

Russell had looked at the pickup truck in the barn briefly as soon as he found out about it. But it wasn't until Tuesday that he had the time to give it a thorough inspection. The hay stacked around had been there so long it had lost its fresh-cut smell. The barn smelled of only of old dust.

The truck, however, looked good, real good. If the odometer was correct it had less than twenty thousand miles on it. The four tires were flat as could be. The interior was like new. The body had no rust. When he asked Liria about it all she said was that Tody came home with it one day and only drove it to town once a week for groceries and other supplies. Other than that it stayed in the barn.

"How did he buy it if he didn't believe in banks?" Russell asked.

"Paid cash."

This made Russell think for a minute. "How did you buy this house without a loan from a bank?"

"Paid cash."

He almost didn't want to ask the next question but he had to, "Where did you get all that cash? Did you bring it from Albania?"

"No, I expect he got it from his brother," she replied walking away.

Russell tried to put these questions out of his mind as he stared at the pickup. It was dark blue. He went around to the driver's side and slid in behind the wheel. It smelled of cigarettes. The keys were in the ignition. He pulled the lever to pop open the hood. Walking around to the front he cautiously opened it.

There was a straight six, a good engine, and it looked like it had been taken care of at least up until two years ago. Russell grabbed a wrench from the bench and removed the battery. Closing the hood, he walked around to the side, knelt by a tire and jotted down the size on a small slip of paper. Then he realized he'd have to take all four wheels in so he crumpled up the paper and tossed it aside. He looked around and found some cinder blocks. Getting out the jack from the truck, he proceeded to remove each wheel. He placed the vehicle up on blocks until he could get the new tires put on.

Russell went into town to look for a local mechanic. He wanted someone everyone knew and trusted, not just one of the franchises. Passing by Betty's Diner he noticed the Edsel out front, so he stopped in. He was met by a familiar welcoming aroma of fresh pie.

"Hey can you recommend a good mechanic and tire shop?" he asked Dave.

"Ferndale Tire Shop. Steve there is the best on both accounts; he does my Edsel."

"Thanks, I found the pickup. it was behind a stack of straw bales and under a canvas tarp. Almost like he was trying to hide it."

"He might have been." replied Dave, then added, "It's almost deer season. Be on the lookout for your neighbor, Greg. He's been known to poach a deer every year off your property. He likes to hunt without a license. I had to run him in a few times. If I have nothing better to do on opening day, I'll be out at your place trying to get him again. See you soon."

As he was leaving a man about his age came through the door.

"Giblets!" Several people cried out. Then one asked, "Where have you been working?"

The man smiled and said, "At the window factory, but I quit, it was a real pain."

As Russell left, the crowd chuckled. It took a few seconds for him to catch the joke.

He found the Ferndale Tire Shop and, sticking out from under a Volkswagen bug, he found Steve. The man looked to be in his late sixties, with a long, gray, straggly goatee. What hair he had left on his head was streaked with grease.

"I've got four tires in my trunk that need replacing," he said after Steve had slid out from under the car. Steve followed him out the front door to where he had parked. Steve took a look at the tires and grabbing two, carried them into the shop.

"You must be the man that bought Shihini's old place," said Steve as the tires were placed on a rack.

"You're right. How did you know?"

"Those are the tires I put on Tody's '64 pickup four, maybe five years ago," Steve said, stepping behind the counter and starting to write up a slip.

"Wow, you have a good memory," remarked Russell.

"Well it was a very memorable tire change," said Steve rummaging through a jar of odds and ends.

"How so?"

"Well, it was the first time I ever tried to patch a tire that had a bullet hole in it," said Steve and he dropped a .22 bullet on the counter in front of Russell. "There, that's what I found inside. I finally convinced him he needed a new set of tires."

There seemed to be more to Mr. Shihini than Russell first thought. If there was more that Steve knew, he didn't say.

"If you just want some basic tires on that truck, I've got a good deal for you. But it'll be maybe tomorrow before I can get them on. That okay with you?" Steve asked.

"Sure, I'm in no hurry, I don't even know if the truck runs. The battery is probably dead. You don't happen to have a charger, do you?"

"If you got it with you I'll put it on the charger overnight."

Russell went back to the car and pulled the battery out of the back seat floor. When he got it in Steve tested the cells. They seemed to be okay so he hooked it up on the charger. With that done, Russell headed back to his car.

Back at the house, he took another look at the truck. Getting a small hand broom he started cleaning out the inside. Once swept, he attacked it with a bucket of warm water and baking soda, trying to remove the cigarette smell. Putting the floor mats back in place after scrubbing them he noticed a little difference in the smell. Then he saw a lump in the driver's seat. Reaching under he pulled out a small phone book that was wedged between the springs and the seat cushion. "Curious," he thought, putting the phone book in his back pocket.

Liria did not have supper ready when he got into the house. What she did have ready was a shopping list.

"We need food," she said simply.

Russell looked at the list and realized she was still planning on cooking the way she did in

Albania. 'This has got to change,' he thought. 'No time like the present.'

Gathering up all his courage he said, "We need to talk about the food you prepare. Not that I'm complaining. I've enjoyed your cooking, but I'm accustomed to other foods too." He let this sink in for a minute. "Is it okay with you that while I'm out I pick up some different food as well? I mean, I could cook up some hamburgers now and then on the grill, or spaghetti and meat sauce."

He paused again watching the expression on her face. It appeared as though she was trying to make a life-changing decision.

"When the hotel was running, we had a cook. One of the things she made was roast beef with potatoes and carrots and onions and I don't know what else. I cannot make roast beef no matter how hard I try. It doesn't taste like the one she made. I would like roast beef again, but I could never fix it. Can you?"

"My mother made the best roast beef I know of, and I have her recipe. I'll get some beef and some other things. But maybe tonight we'll just have some hamburgers, okay?"

Liria smiled and said, "Okay, I am glad you've come; you came at a good time."

"Why, because you miss roast beef?"

"No, because I am now out of money for food. That's why I was hoping the insurance money would come right away, I don't have a penny left."

Russell laughed as he walked out to the car, admiring God's timing of everything.

He pondered the process of turning this place back into a guest house, as he drove along. He had a lot of work to do. He was getting a pickup truck. That would help, but this place was built some time ago and needed some updating.

Once back home, he grabbed an empty notebook and a measuring tape. The rooms were small by modern standards but usable. The problem was the bathrooms. There were not enough of them. "People want their own bathrooms nowadays.", he thought. His solution was to use one room, splitting it to make two small bathrooms for the rooms on either side of them.

He needed to see if he could run the plumbing and fit everything in. It took him most of the evening and he was getting tired when he decided to put away his things and finish up in the morning. One thing for certain, he was going to need help. "How can I afford a team of carpenters to do all this?", he wondered.

In the morning he had an idea, but his thoughts were interrupted by a brown pickup truck pulling into the yard. He recognize the owner when he got out of the driver's seat.

"What brings you to my neck of the woods?" asked Russell shaking his hand.

"Your tires are done. I thought I'd just pop over and take a look at this old pick up again," said Steve.

"Shouldn't you be running your shop?"

"Seeing that I own the place I don't think I'll get fired for opening up an hour late," smiled Steve.

Russell noticed he'd brought a jack with him, so between the two of them they put the tires back on. Then Steve got the battery out of the back of the truck and hooked it up. Disconnecting the distributor cap, he gave the engine a few turns and let it sit.

"That's to get some oil in the cylinders before we try starting this thing," he explained. Then he added, "You got any coffee in that house?"

"Should have, how do you like it?"

"Too thick to sip and too thin to plow... and black."

Russell went to the house to grab the coffee. By the time he'd come back, Steve had the truck running.

Steve had chugged down half his cup before commenting, "She runs pretty good. I'd take it easy, no long trips for a while, but you got yourself a pretty good little pickup."

"What do I owe you?" asked Russell.

"I don't know, stop by the shop sometime and we'll settle up. I mostly wanted to come out and see the old place. Liria still here?"

"Yup, she came with the place and I don't think anything anyone says could make her move until she is ready."

"You going to open it up or live here by yourself?"

"Well, I don't know what it will actually become, but my goal is to have a guesthouse for missionaries. I've served overseas long enough to know a lot of people that could use a place like this when they get stateside. I figure I'm close enough to Chicago O'Hare that it would be a convenient place to stop for a day or two. Missionaries need some R&R when they get home," explained Russell.

"Missionaries?" Steve laughed, "That'll be a far cry from what used to come here!"

"What do you mean?"

"Well, I only know about folks from the cars they drive. From what I've seen and what my dad told me, the folks that stayed here had mighty funny cars. Hidden compartments in their trunks, extra gas tanks that smelled like whiskey and engines that could outrun anything the police had. Well, I best be going." Steve got back in his truck. Leaning out the window he added, "be on the lookout for your neighbor Greg. He likes to hunt on your land but doesn't like to get a hunting license. He's not dangerous, just cheap." And with that, he headed out.

"Interesting," thought Russell.

Liria was hanging up laundry when he walked back to the house. "By the way," he asked, "what kind of business did Tody's brother have?"

"Oh, you know, the family business," she answered picking up the basket and heading into the house.

"Interesting family," thought Russell.

After lunch, Russell placed a call to his friend in Chicago who organized youth work teams.

"Listen, Andy," he started after the customary greetings, "do you ever have a team ready to go and something falls through? If so I could use a team here now and then." Then he took the time to explain where he was living and what he was hoping to do.

"Sounds like a legitimate project. I'd be glad to send you a team. Things like that happen all the time and it's nice to have something in my back pocket. Why don't you send me a list of what you need to have done and I'll see if I get any takers." said Andy.

"I'd appreciate it! I'll have some materials on hand so I could deal with a team on short notice," Russell thanked him.

Having solved two problems in one day put Russell in a good mood. He jumped in the pickup, drove to town, paid the bill at Steve's and bought a quart of ice cream and some bananas. It was the first banana split Liria had had in her entire life.

The next day he was in town picking up some supplies and notice the Edsel parked in front of Betty's. He went in and got a cup of coffee and joined Dave at his table.

"What do you know about Mr. Shihini and the kind of people that would frequent his hotel?" he asked quietly.

"I've heard stories, but you can't arrest a man on rumors."

Russell then showed him the phone book that he had pulled out of the truck. Dave looked at it for a few minutes.

"Can I keep this for a few days? I'd like to run some of these names and dates by a few friends of mine," said Dave.

"Sure. I'll let you know if I find anything else." He reached for his bill, but Dave grabbed it first.

"Official business expense," explained Dave, still looking at the phone book.

It was Friday afternoon when the Edsel pulled into Russell's yard. Dave got out and leaned against the car waiting for Russell to meet him there.

"Does Liria know anything about that phonebook?" he asked.

"Never asked. Why what's in it?"

"Enough names and dates to put somebody away for a long time."

"Who? Liria?" Russell asked unbelievingly.

"No, her nephew," Dave paused for a minute, "I need your help to ask Liria about Tody's brother. He passed away a few years back, but there's a lot in there about his son, Liria's nephew. The mafia may have been using this place as a stopover between Chicago and Detroit. I don't know how involved Tody was or how much Liria knows. See if you can figure that out, okay?"

"I'll see what I can do."

And at that, Dave got back into his car and drove away. Liria was sweeping the porch when Russell walked back to the house. Knowing her, Russell thought it best to be direct and to the point.

"Liria," he said as he eased into a deck chair, "Dave thinks that your brother-in-law and nephew were involved in some illegal activities. I'm sorry you have to find out about this, but we need to know what you do. Did you ever suspect that illegal things were happening here at the Inn?

Liria just looked at Russell with an unbelieving smile. "But Mr. Green, I told you, they were in the family business, the family business." Liria walked over to Russell and put a hand on his shoulder. "Tody was not the first man to get buried in the backyard."

CHAPTER FOUR

Russell stayed on the porch letting this new bit of information sink into his brain. Liria, knowing a longer talk was coming, made a pot of tea in the kitchen and sat down to wait for him. The tea had steeped long enough by the time Russell came in from the porch. With a sigh, Russell sank into a chair and poured himself a cup.

Without looking up from her teacup Liria asked, "Do I go to jail now?"

"Not if Dave and I have anything to do with it. But we will need to know more information and just what was going on here," answered Russell.

Liria leaned back, trying to decide what to say, how much to trust this man that had just bought her house, who had found money for her to live on the rest of her life, who had gotten her husband's truck running again and who now had found out a secret that she had hoped was buried with her husband. She decided to start at the beginning.

"I do not know when I was born; the year or the day. It was not our custom to record the birth of girls. My father was a Muslim but never attended a mosque. As he could not read, he never read the Koran. The sum total of his religion was counting his prayer beads. My mother was a Christian. She would light candles now and then on certain days or when she had certain prayers she needed to say, but the only other thing she did was to count her prayer beads.

Our family lived in a tiny village called Gurdeti. We had a small farm, goats, a cow, chickens and a garden where we grew vegetables. We were like everybody else, nobody was different, we were all poor but because we had nobody to compare with, we didn't know that.

"In the winter things were hard and there were weeks and weeks where we ate nothing but dried beans. In the spring and fall, our fields were full of mud. In the winter the fields were full of cold mud. Through the middle of the town ran our river. It was not much more than a creek, and very polluted. We would all throw our trash into that creek, hoping it would wash away. But it would pile up and rot and stink. Only when the floods came in the spring did the river run halfway clean. But then it would overflow its banks and deposit our trash back at our doorstep.

"I had an older brother, of whom the family was very proud. He would grow up to take over the farm and to take care of mother and father. My parents loved my brother very much, but because my little sister and I were girls, we were not loved like that.

The big excitement of the week was Market Day. We would dress up in our best clothes and walk into the main part of town, less than a mile, to sell or trade the vegetables we had extra.

"It wasn't until I was fourteen or so that I realized how poor we were and that for a girl the only hope was to marry outside of the village.

"As soon as he could, my father started to look for a husband for me. One day when I was about fifteen years old, a man came into the village dressed in fine clothes. He had a pocket watch on a silver chain. He stayed in the village a few days talking with people and spending money. We were all very impressed.

"On the third day, he came to our house. After a few minutes of talking with this man, my father told me to make coffee. It was then that I knew I was engaged. As soon as the man and my father were finished with their coffee, I was pledged to marry that man. No papers, no rings, no asking me for my opinion, just a cup of coffee, and the rest of my life was planned. He would come back in one month to pick me up and take me away forever.

"Finally my father was happy with me, for he was able to get a very large brideprice. My mother was frantic. So much had to be done in the next month! Making clothes, sheets, and pillowcases; everything that I would need to set up a house.

"After three weeks of hard work, my life changed again. A girl came back to the village alone and pregnant. This was a great shame for her family. She had been married off a year before and had left the village in great fanfare. As she had been a friend of mine in school, I went to talk to her. She told me that the man she married had married several other girls that same summer. He had put them all into a large van and brought them to Italy. There he sold them to a brothel. She was told that she had to pay back her brideprice. When they found out she was pregnant, she was of no more use to them. They sent her to a hospital to get an abortion, but on the way she escaped and made her way back home, earning the money the only way she knew how.

"I told my friend about my upcoming marriage and showed her a picture of my fiancé. She recognized the man but called him by a different name. I almost fainted. I brought my friend back to my house and told her story to my parents.

My mother was speechless but my father called her a liar. He said, whatever happens, is not up to him, he had drunk coffee with a man, the deal was set, I belonged to that man and whatever he wanted to do with me was up to him. No longer was I a daughter to my father. Going back on an agreed-upon marriage would shame my father too much. It did not matter that I would be a prostitute in a foreign country. Nobody would know of that, but not going through with an agreed-upon marriage was too much shame for our family.

"My friend had already brought much shame to the village. Many people were urging her parents to kill her, to bring back honor to the family. Late the next night she left for the capital city, never to be heard from again, never even to be talked of again, except in whispered gossip.

"The next week was the worst week of my life. I begged and I pleaded but to no avail. My father was still set on marrying me off to a man who would sell me as a prostitute. My father said it wasn't true, that my husband had a good job and that I would be happy and safe. He said he had known of him for a long time; that he was an honest man.

"The day my future husband was to arrive, news came to the town that he had been murdered. That same evening another man showed up at our door. He was an acquaintance of my father; one he had done business with. He talked with my father behind closed doors for at least half an hour. Then my father again called me to make coffee.

"When I brought the coffee in I looked at my future husband for the first time in my life. Mr. Tody Shihini was about thirty years old. He smiled at me. My father explained he had a good job and needed to travel to a place called America. I'd never heard of America. He had to leave in one month and he would take me with him. Because I still didn't even have a birth certificate, we would have to leave that night to go into the big town nearby to get a paper to prove I was born. The next day we would have to go to the capital to start the paperwork to get a passport. All this meant that I would have to leave with him now, as his wife.

"That afternoon the imam was not available but the priest was. So that is how we had a Christian wedding. After the wedding, my bags were loaded in a borrowed car. I left my home town for the first time in my life."

All the time Liria was talking, Russell sat listening. But Liria had gotten up and started to prepare food. She worked subconsciously, making food from her childhood. To work with her hands seemed to help her to talk. Byrek, a bean salad and then yet another salad made with tomatoes and cucumbers and onions all flowed from her hands. She served it as soon as it was ready, and they began to eat without a pause in her story.

"In the big city of Tirana, I mostly stayed in our room. I was afraid of all the people and the cars on the road. The month passed quickly and soon we were heading to the seaport town to get on a boat to take us to Italy. From there we boarded a large steamer and left for America.

"Everything was so new to me. I was homesick most of the time but that was also combined with the thrill of being so far away from home. I did not know what to expect from being married; I did not know how to be a wife. Tody was a kind man and very patient with his new bride."

At this memory, Liria smiled.

"It wasn't until New York City was in view, that he told me about his job. His family was in the Mafia. His brother was in charge of something in Chicago and a cousin worked in Detroit. These cities were just names to me at the time. I had no idea how big America was. His job was to operate an inn halfway between the two. It was to be run as a legitimate business, but also as a place where secrets could be kept. Tody was chosen because he had no heart for the rougher more illegal aspects of the business. For this I was thankful.

"He also told me some other news that changed my world. My father was also a part of the business. Not a part of the family, but he ran errands for them. One errand was to find girls to sell as prostitutes in Italy."

Liria sank in her chair as the memory hit her again. Russell watched as a solitary tear rolled down her face.

"He knew what he was doing when engaged me to that man. It was he that arranged my friend to be sold in Italy. How many others? I do not know. I hope I never find out."

Liria took a sip of her tea and continued talking.

"After New York we took a train to Chicago where Tody's brother picked us up and brought us to this place. Here we made a home. It was in this kitchen that I was finally able to make a meal for my husband! We kept chickens and a goat. I planted quite a large garden at first but over the years it became smaller. We tried to have children but they never came. We stayed very busy with legitimate business, as well as family business, and many times I did not know which was which. There were times though when the blood had to be washed out from the sheets and bullet holes had to be patched in the walls."

Russell interrupted her, "Please do not tell me any details that would get you in trouble."

"One more thing then," she added, "after the first death at the inn, I asked Tody if he had ever killed a man. He told me only one. He had killed the first man that I was to marry."

The shock of this information took Russell's breath away. A man could kill another man, and then, on that same day marry his fiancée.

"Tody had known what the man was up to. He had also been admiring me for some time and did not want me to end up in that line of work. So he did the only thing that he thought would work. He took a big risk, killing another member of the Family, but nobody found out. You are the first person other than myself and Tody to know."

Liria looked as if a weight lifted from her shoulders.

"When new highways and faster cars came, fewer people needed to stop here. We could not afford to keep up the whole place, so we let some rooms go and only maintained three or four for guests.

"Tody's brother died in an accident. I think his son, my nephew, took over his place, but I don't know. I tried to stay away from the family side of the business. I reasoned that I could not tell a secret I did not know. For the love of my husband, I did not want to reveal anything that would get him in trouble. I think the family just forgot about us."

"Do you ever keep in touch with your other family? I mean your sister or your brother?" asked Russell.

"I've written to my sister now and again, but these last few years I am forgetting some Albanian and my little sister is having a hard time reading. My parents are gone, my brother has died, I don't even know if there is a town left called Gurdeti."

"Tell me more about your town," asked Russell.

"I miss my town." said Liria with a smile, "Even the mud. I loved feeding my chickens and collecting eggs, bringing them to market on market day. If we sold a lot of fruits and vegetables and my chickens had many eggs we could each buy a piece of candy! I miss looking up and seeing the mountains on three sides of our valley. I miss hearing the cows talk to each other early in the morning from farm to farm. As a little girl, I imagined that they were telling the secrets of their owners and I wished that I could learn their language. Mostly I miss my little sister. She was married to a man from the village but he died young. I am not sure anymore exactly where she lives. It's been two years since we've written. Maybe she has gone too."

"I have friends who live in Tirana. I can have them stop in and check in on her. Would you like that?"

"If you like. She may not be easy to find."

The rest of the day Liria was lost in memories. She went about the house cooking and cleaning with her mind in a country far away. Russell caught up on e-mails and jotted one to his friends in Albania.

As he crawled into bed it seemed to Russell that he was collecting impossible things to do: fix up this house, prevent Liria from going to jail, and find her sister.

CHAPTER FIVE

Waiting was hard but Russell knew he had let Dave do his job. There was enough around the house to keep him busy. He was drawing up a master plan for the old inn. He also made material lists and occasionally picked things up to have on hand.

In the back of Russell's mind was the reminder that this Saturday morning deer season opened, and he had a neighbor that would be armed and encroaching on his land. He could just let him do it, and then let Dave arrest him. He could put up a fence, but that would cost too much. He didn't think a 'no trespassing' sign would keep Greg out. So he decided on a little more information. He started with a simple internet search.

"Liria," Russell asked Monday morning over breakfast, "did Tody ever go hunting on the property here?"

Liria responded by saying something in Albanian that, judging by the tone, Russell was glad he didn't understand.

"That man," she continued in English, "he spent so much money on this gun and that gun for hunting and every year he spent money to get a license to hunt. Then he spent money on clothes for hunting. He even built a deer out of wood to practice shooting at!"

Here she again slipped into Albanian for a few choice words. Then taking a deep breath she continued back in English. "But did he ever bring meat to the table? Did he ever shoot one and bring a roast for me to cook with potatoes and carrots?"

She was staring at Russell expecting an answer, so Russell just shrugged his shoulders.

"Not once!"

With that Liria stormed out of the kitchen and into her room.

Obviously, a sore subject thought Russell. He thought the wisest thing would be to disappear for a few hours, and headed off to Betty's.

As he walked in he was passed by a man walking out the door, wearing a surgical mask.

"Who was that?" he asked Dave who was sitting at his usual table.

"That is Giblets McDonald, said a man at the table.

"Macintosh," corrected another man.

"McGraff," said Dave in an authoritative voice.

Russell then remembered him from the other day.

"Why the mask? Is he sick?"

"He's got a cold," said the first man at the table.

"The flu," corrected the other man.

"He says he's heard there is a flu going around and he is afraid of catching it," said Dave. "He comes in now and then with a pretty good joke about where he's been working. Today he said he'd started a funeral home."

"Yeah, but he had to quit because business was dead," interrupted the men at the table.

"So what do I need to go hunting this year?" Russell asked Dave.

"Three things: a license, a gun, and common sense. Since I think you already have the third one you should head over to the sporting goods store and get yourself a license," said Dave.

"What kind of gun do most people use around here?"

"Well, I don't deer hunt much myself, but the last deer that I shot I did with my .45."

"You went hunting with a pistol?"

"It was an easy shot, he was in the grocery store," said Dave nonchalantly.

Russell said nothing but gave his best you-better-tell-me-more stare.

"This twelve-point buck was wandering around in traffic. He got scared by a big truck and ran through the big open double doors of the grocery store. He made quite a mess. I waited until he calmed down by the fruits and vegetables. The meat department butchered him for free and the whole town had a barbecue the next Saturday. That buck made a lot of burgers."

At the sporting goods store he learned that new regulations required a class before a hunting license was given, but because of his age, he would be grandfathered in. Gratefully he paid for his hunting license, then swung by the tire shop. Steve was trying to squeeze himself into the engine compartment of a Yugo.

"I've been thinking of doing some deer hunting this year. Wondering what kind of guns people use around here. Dave recommends his .45, but only if I'm to hunt in the supermarket."

Steve smiled remembering the year of the buck barbecue.

"Yes, that was some party. People added a few more deer to the mix. They closed down Main Street for the day and set up tables and tents. They charged a buck a burger, a buck a beer or soda, and a buck for ice cream. We raised enough money to remodel the health clinic. But as to your question, most people around here use a twelve-gauge with a slug. That's what I'd recommend for your woods. Not much for distance, but you don't want that, as close as you are to town."

"Is that what my neighbor Greg would use?"

"That's all he's got."

"And is that what you use?"

"Nope," said Steve, "I don't use a gun. I only bow hunt. I already got one deer this year. My average is three."

Armed with this new information, Russell headed back to his house. What he found there was a much subdued Liria and a travel trunk in the middle of the sitting room.

"Good, you're home," said Liria, wiping her hands on her apron. "Come." She pushed him into the living room.

"After Tody died, I took all his guns and put them in here, along with all his hunting gear. If you are going to hunt, you may use whatever you find. Just try to bring back some meat." With that, she left Russell to examine the contents of the trunk.

On the top was a bright orange hunting vest with hat and gloves to match. Next was a camouflage suit that just might fit him. Underneath, wrapped individually in old sheets, were the guns. The first one he pulled out was a .357 bolt-action rifle with a scope.

The next one made Russell smile. Evidently, Tody did his homework too. It was a twelve-gauge pump with interchangeable barrels, one for shot and one for a slug. There were two other guns wrapped up: a nine-millimeter Smith & Wesson and a 38 special. Obviously, hunting wasn't the only thing on Tody's mind.

At the bottom of the trunk was an assortment of ammunition for each weapon. The shotgun had the most. Not only were there slugs and shot but also shells filled with rock salt. The man clearly viewed self-defense as more important than hunting.

Grabbing his notebook, Russell copied down the serial numbers and information about each gun then he called Dave.

"So how does one go about getting a gun permit in this town?"

"You should have filed those papers when you bought your gun," explained Dave.

"I didn't buy one, Tody has several here and I thought I'd better get them registered in my name. I don't think Liria will use them."

"What did he have?"

"A twelve-gauge, a .357 bolt action rifle, a nine-millimeter Smith & Wesson and a thirty-eight special."

"Wow, the man was armed. Well, I'll run a background check on you, then you should probably come in and get checked out with the handguns, how about Wednesday afternoon?"

"I'll be there." And he hung up.

Wednesday afternoon he arrived at the police station with all his guns. A deputy took the guns from him and ushered him down the stairs to a waiting room. He could hear popping sounds from what he assumed was a firing range. Twenty minutes later the same deputy appeared with a stack of papers.

"None of the guns you surrendered were stolen or wanted as evidence. We have no reason to believe that they were gotten illegally or with malicious intent. Therefore once you check out with the handguns, you will be free to take them home. You will not have a permit to carry a concealed weapon." The deputy went on to give him an hour-long instruction in gun safety. He then looked at his watch, motioning for Russell to follow him into the next room.

It was a firing range, and on the table were his two handguns. He was handed hearing protection and eyeglasses and told simply to try and hit the target. Russell had never fired a real gun before in his life. There had been BB guns and the occasional old .22, but this was different. Summoning up the memories of every Western he'd seen, he planted his feet squarely, took a breath, aimed and pulled the trigger. Nothing happened. He tried it again but this time remembered to release the safety.

He surprised himself by being able to put three bullets close to the center of the target. He was better with a nine-millimeter than with the .38 special. The officer explained that typically the .38 was not as accurate. The officer signed some papers, made Russell sign on several lines, then packed the guns back into the bag that he brought them in and wished him a good day.

Walking out of the police station he wondered how it could be so easy. But then remembered that Dave had already run his background check to make it easier for him. That thought was going to make it harder to do what he was planning on doing on Saturday morning.

Friday was spent wandering through his woods. He enjoyed the fragrance of birch, oak, and pine. This was a mature forest.

His alarm was set for 4:00 am, but he was up by 3:30. He was enjoying a cup of coffee when he noticed the Edsel pulling up into his driveway with the lights off. Dave quietly got out and walked into his woods. Dressed in his orange vest and orange hat, and carrying the shotgun Russell made his way to the spot he'd picked out the day before. At 5:01 a shot rang out. Leaping to his feet he started running and shouting.

"I got him, I got him. Greg, Greg, did you see that? I got him!" Russell shouted time and time again.

As soon as he got to where the deer had fallen, he handed his gun to the stranger that was standing there, pulled out his license, and tagged the deer. His smile was beaming as wide as it could when he looked up into the faces of a very surprised neighbor and an even more surprised Chief of Police.

Dave bent over and examined the tag. He got up slowly and looking at Russell square in the face he asked, "Is this your deer?"

Russell looked Dave squarely back in the eye and said, "That's my deer."

Dave looked at Greg who simply shrugged his shoulders. Dave looked back at Russell, then he turned and walked back to his car.

When Dave was out of earshot, Greg set the guns against a tree and said quietly, "That ain't your deer."

"My land, my tag, my deer," was all Russell said.

"Mister, what're you trying to do here? Who the heck you think you are?"

"First off, my name is Russell Green, I'm your new neighbor," said Russell sticking out his hand. When his neighbor did not take his hand, he dropped it and continued, "Chief May was out here to arrest you and put you behind bars for at least a month. I just saved you jail time."

"So you're going to take my deer?"

Russell sat down a tree stump. "No you can have it, however, Liria would like a roast."

With that much settled Greg pulled out a large knife and started to field dress the deer.

"Why don't you ever get a license?" Russell asked.

"My daddy never needed a license and I don't see why I need one now. It's a free country and I've been hunting for years. This used to be all our land before those Shihinis got a hold of it. To me, it's a matter of principle."

Russell was distracted with the ease that Greg gutted the deer.

"You are a real artist," he said.

Greg looked at him like he was crazy.

"I mean with that deer, the way you field dressed it so quick, I could never do that."

"Been doing it since I was ten. My daddy showed me how, not too far from where I am right now. That was back when this was all our land. His daddy had learned from great granddaddy back when they first came to this part of the world. That field over there is where they cleared the trees for their first crop." He pointed with the bloodied knife to the field behind Russell's house. He paused, then, pointing with a bloody thumb toward his house he said, "They used the logs to build the cabin." Then he quickly changed the subject, "If you follow me, I'll get you your roast."

Russell picked up the rifles and followed him into the garage that had been added on to the original log cabin. Greg hoisted the deer and within minutes handed Russell a nice roast in a plastic shopping bag.

"Thank you. Liria will be pleased," said Russell then set it down and leaned against the workbench. "Do you ever go hunting out of season?"

"No, I ain't that stupid. Maybe with a bow, you could sneak a deer out of the woods as Steve does, but I ain't no bow hunter and if people start hearing gunshots out of season there's sure to be some snoop'n around."

"But you won't get a license," Russell said this as a statement, not a question.

"I told you, s'matter of principle."

"I can admire that," said Russell, "I'm a man of principle too so maybe we can reach an agreement, neighbor to neighbor. I can see why you have a beef against Mr. Shihini, but he's dead and I bought this land fair and square. My principle is, I don't want any illegal hunting on my property. So here's my offer, every year I'll buy you a license. In exchange, you give me a couple of roasts for Liria to cook up." Russell waited for this idea to sink in. "We got a deal?"

"And if I don't?" asked Greg without looking up from the deer.

"I'll let Chief May run you in and you can do your time."

"Is he your friend?"

"Maybe not anymore after what I did to him this morning."

Greg continued cutting, expertly butchering the fresh meat. "There's a new buck that's been coming around. Must be a six-point,; looks like he'd have a good roast on him."

"I can get to that license this afternoon," said Russell, "if we have a deal."

"Deal." Said Greg slapping another steak in Russell's bag.

Liria was more than happy with the meat but Russell knew that Dave was not. He thought he would go down and try to explain things to his friend in the afternoon, but he didn't have to wait that long. Before noon the official police car pulled up in front of his house.

Russell saw the fear in Liria's eyes and comforted her by saying, "He's come to get me not you."

He walked out to the car and noticed that Dave was not looking at him.

"Morning Dave, I was going to come down to your office and have a chat later on."

"I ought to run you in," Dave said, still not looking at him.

"Sorry, but I think I can explain."

"I thought preachers were not supposed to lie."

"I didn't lie, and I'm a retired missionary, not a preacher."

"That wasn't your deer."

"It was on my land."

Dave was quiet for a few minutes. "I checked the books. Legally you are right, but I thought you were the law abiding type. If you would rather be friends with those that break the law then those that make the law I guess that's your right."

"He's not a lawbreaker," said Russell quietly.

"He hunts without a license," said Dave plainly.

"Not any more."

"Explain," said Dave finally turning to look at him.

"Greg doesn't break the law in any other area. He has a permit for the gun, he pays his taxes, he's not wanted for any other crime, he just feels that the land still belongs to his family. His link, perhaps his only link, with his ancestors is his ability to hunt on that property as his great-grandfather did. Now I don't mind his hunting on my land but I do mind him not having a license. So we made a deal.

"I knew I could not get him to make a deal unless I first got on his good side. Even if that meant being on your bad side for a while. I'm going to buy him a license every year, and from every deer he gets, I get some of the meat. This way, he gets to hunt without spending money on a license, Liria gets to cook her famous roast with potatoes and carrots, I get to eat it and you get to keep your jail cell empty."

"I think I still got the short end of the stick," said Dave after a long pause.

"So how could we make this deal better for you?"

"When Liria cooks that roast, invite me to dinner."

"Are you free Wednesday night?" asked Russell.

"I'll be here. Now I think I've kept the mayor waiting long enough. I've got my monthly report to hand in." Dave said as he held out his hand to Russell. They smiled as they shook hands.

When Russell went back into the house it was obvious from Liria's expression that she had been holding her breath most of the time that he and Dave talking out front.

"Who is going to jail?" Liria asked.

"Nobody. That's the beauty of it, and Dave is going to join us for dinner on Wednesday when you cook that roast."

"What?! The Chief of Police at my table?! Me, serving food to the Chief of Police, in this place?!"

"Sure, why not?"

"My husband will turn over in his grave!" exclaimed Liria.

"He already did that, remember?"

"Oh yes," said Liria much relieved as she went about her business.

CHAPTER SIX

Russell woke up one morning and wanted a boat. He was not sure where the idea came from. He was not sure if there were any boats for sale in Ferndale. Liria could not help. As she could not swim she stayed far away from water.

"What you need to do, is go see Charlie." They all told him down at Betty's when he stopped in for some advice. "You have to wait till about 8:30 before you try to talk to Charlie. He doesn't own a timepiece. He gets up when Amtrak rolls past his house at eight o'clock. This triggers his coffee and bowl of Cheerios. You don't want to talk to him until he's finished at least two cups of coffee."

Russell had just heard the train pull through, so he thought he'd better wait a while before he made his appearance. He stopped off at the bank and pulled out some extra cash. He felt he would get a better deal if he flashed the green stuff.

As Russel drove south, he knew why he had never seen Charlie's before. It was behind the granary next to the railroad tracks. The gate was open, so he pulled his truck in. He parked just inside the entrance because there was no other space for his truck. By the looks of the vines crawling on the gate, he assumed it had not been closed in the last five to ten years. Then he glanced around the yard at Charlie's boats.

Charlie had boats like a dog had fleas. They were of every size and description. Some were piled on top of each other. Some were in the process of being put together while others were in the process of being taken apart. It was hard to tell which way they were going.

There was one forty-foot yacht sitting up in a cradle in all its glory and majesty. The cabin and decks appeared to be sound and in good shape. The sides looked like they almost had a new coat of paint. The boat only had one visible problem as far as he could tell. Below the waterline, the boat was, well, not there. His fascination with how the yacht was sitting on the cradle without a hull below the waterline was interrupted by a scruffy man holding what Russell hoped was his second cup of coffee.

"I'll let you have it for a real good deal," said Charlie.

"Actually I'm looking more for something I can go fishing in," said Russell, "something that would hopefully fit in the back of my truck so I don't need a trailer."

"Are you particular about what it's made of?"

"Not really, just so that I can handle it myself, putting it in and pulling it out."

Charlie thought a few minutes then said, "Well, follow me, let's see what's out there."

For the next hour, Charlie brought Russell over the entire lot, pulling out boats here and there, listing the pluses and drawbacks of each one. He always ended each boat interview with it's price. How Charlie could remember the details of the fleet was more than Russell could figure out.

In the end, Russell chose the eight-foot aluminum pram. He did not choose the outboard engine. He figured he would get by rowing. He did not want the extra noise and figured he could use the exercise. They hauled the boat over to his truck and loaded it up. Then they went into the office to finish the deal.

The office was a cross between a living room and a junkyard. A small black-and-white television was on a morning news program, but thankfully the volume was low. The place smelled of grease. There was a couch that held stacks of old newspapers and magazines. At a glance, Russell noticed that the most recent seemed about seven years old. There were bits and pieces of boats and engines in piles around the outside edge of the room. Although nothing was labeled, there seemed to be an order and system to the piles. The table that served as Charlie's desk was remarkably free of papers. It did have it's a collection of tools and motor parts and in the center, the empty cereal bowl.

Charlie bent over a milk crate on the floor. It was filled with an array of colorful files. He pulled a few sheets from various files. "Since you're not going to put a motor on it, the paperwork is a lot easier," he said, grabbing a pen from a jar on the table.

Russell watched him put the number '8' in a blank next to the word 'foot' and a checkmark in the box next to the word 'aluminum'. At the bottom of the sheet, there was a blank for the purchase price. Charlie very carefully wrote the number '100' just in front of a decimal point with two zeros.

"I hope you brought cash. I don't deal with checks nor cards and life's too short for IOUs," said Charlie.

Russell opened up his wallet and handed him a crisp hundred dollar bill. Then he leaned over and signed his name in the box where Charlie was pointing. Charlie then made a copy of the bill of sale and stamped both copies "Paid".

They shook hands and Russell went out to take his boat home. On the way, he stopped at the local hardware store. He breathed in the unique aroma of paint and live bait. Charlie had thrown in an anchor and some oars, but he needed lines and a life jacket.

"I see you've been to Charlie's," the clerk said as Russell got his cart. "He doesn't do much business these days, now that the new marina has opened up in the next town. Still, I suppose he gets by."

Curious, Russell asked, "When did the marina open up?"

"Oh, 'bout seven years ago."

"And how long has Charlie been in business?"

The clerk had to think for a minute. "Can't remember a time when he wasn't there, come to think of it. You'll have to ask somebody else that question."

His next stop was the sporting goods aisle. He needed a fishing pole and some tackle. He probably should get a fishing license and make it all legal.

"What do you recommend that I get for fishing around here?" he asked the clerk.

"You better let Pop set you up," the man replied, then yelled into the back room, "Hey, Pop, got a guy here that wants to know how to go fish'n." Then he went back to stocking the shelves.

An older gentleman came in from the back room. His uniform shirt had the name "Pop" over the pocket.

The next half hour was an education in the benefits of different rods and reels, just what kind of fish you could find in the lakes around the area, where and when you should fish, and what bait they like best. It was hard to try and remember everything that Pop said, but Russell figured he could stop by and ask again. Pop even helped him with his fishing license, carefully filling out the form in perfect penmanship. It reminded Russell of Charlie's form.

"Say, any idea how long Charlie's been in business?" Russell figured he might know.

Pop got real thoughtful, then said, "He was probably thirteen or fourteen when he started fixing boats in his daddy's backyard. His mama died a few years before that and he and his dad moved into that shack next to the railroad tracks. His daddy took his mama's death real hard. It turned him mean. Most folks around here felt that Charlie might be getting more than his fair share of lickkins.

"Then Charlie's daddy took to drink, lost his job and died young. It was probably a good thing for Charlie. He was pretty good with his hands and kept on making boats, fixing up old ones and repairing engines. Keeps to himself." Pop paused as if trying to think if there is anything else he had to say about Charlie. "He will always give you a good deal and he's honest and fair."

By this time they had picked out a rod and reel and some tackle to go with it. It seemed that the shopping lasted as long as the story and when Pop ran out of things to say about

Charlie, he also ran out of things to sell to Russell. He rang up the bill, wished him a good day and headed for the back room.

Russell went home to think. There was something about the day's activity that suggested a bigger story than the one he had been told. He wondered if the library could give him more information than he got from Pop.

That afternoon he spent a good two hours poring over old newspapers in the musty basement of the local library. The papers were all there and had not been transferred onto microfilm or digitalized. For some reason, that fact made his quest more mysterious. He found what he was looking for.

That evening, as he was looking through the bookshelves at home, he asked Liria, "When did you learn English? Did you ever go to school here?"

Liria looked as if she had just swallowed a bitter lemon. "Oh don't remind me of those days," she shook her head sadly. "All during the boat trip Tody kept trying to teach me what little English he knew. Then once when we got here, a man came and tried to teach me

English, but he didn't know much more than Tody did.

"Finally they put me in this school. It was at night. There were many other people from different countries there. The teacher was kind and very helpful. She gave me some wonderful books with pictures that helped me understand the words. Slowly I learned. It was a very happy day when I went to the store by myself for the first time and was able to read the labels on the cans and communicate with the store owner."

Russell noticed Liria was smiling again.

"Those are my books there," she said pointing to the top shelf.

Russell reached up and went through the books. He made a pile on the table of books pulled off from various shelves. He went to the room that he was starting to set up as his office. He pulled some papers out of his files and made several copies. He drifted off to sleep trying to recall the different piles around Charlie's office.

He left home shortly after he heard the train pull through town in the morning. He wanted to catch Charlie early. As he walked into the office, Charlie had just finished pouring his second cup of coffee.

"What can I do for you? You need another boat?" laughed Charlie as he sat down behind the table.

"No, I just had a question about this document somebody gave me about boating in this area. What do they mean here in this first sentence?" asked Russell pointing to the top line of a sheet of paper.

Russell noticed that Charlie never looked down at the paper.

"Well what do you think it means?" asked Charlie sounding a little flustered.

"Well I've read it a few times and I can't make it out. What would you think it says?" pressed Russell still looking at Charlie's eyes.

"Well if you can't figure it out, how in the world am I supposed to know?" answered Charlie.

Russell sat down in the chair that was across the table from Charlie. He waited a few seconds.

"You can't read, can you?"

Charlie slunk down deeper into his chair and his head hung forward.

"I can help you," Russell said with a smile. "I have helped many people learn to read, people from many different countries, none of them as smart as you."

Charlie was quiet for a while. "I ain't smart, not smart enough to learn to read."

"Who told you that? Your daddy?"

Russell watched as Charlie fought with the answer, seeming to become a ten-year-old boy again.

"Yeah, him, then the teachers too. I finally just quit trying."

Russell looked around the floor and found the piston ring right where he remembered seeing it.

"What's wrong with this?"

Charlie was glad for the change of subject. "Why, that came off Pop's outboard. That man knows a lot about fishing, but he doesn't know diddly about engines. He ran that thing without oil for the longest time. One day just got too hot to run and it froze up."

"How can you tell that?"

"Why shoot, anybody with a lick of sense can tell by the way that ring is worn and misshaped that it hasn't had oil for a good long time."

"If you can read the marks on this ring, you've got enough sense to learn to read the letters in this book," said Russell, placing Liria's first book on his desk.

Charlie looked at the children's book on this table like it was a snake ready to bite him.

"Too late," he finally said.

"Never," countered Russell.

"How did you figure this out?" Charlie asked trying to change the subject again.

"Well, you stopped getting magazines when the customers stopped coming. By the look of the dust on them, you haven't touched them for years. Then there was that fill-in-the-blank form for your bill of sale and your color-coded file system. Pretty slick, no reading needed. But also it was the stories I read in the old newspapers about how your momma died and what Pop told me about your dad," Russell paused to let this sink in, then added, "He probably took his frustration out on you, blaming you for what happened, calling you the stupid one, trying to remove the blame from himself."

Russell looked down to the floor waiting for Charlie to answer.

"It was my fault, I couldn't read the medicine label right, I gave my momma the wrong medicine. They say it was an accident but it was my fault, I was too stupid to read the label right."

Russell figured there were tears in Charlie's eyes but he didn't want to look up to embarrass him.

"Who asked you to read the label?" asked Russell slowly.

Charlie was trying to recall a picture and a memory that he had often tried to forget.

"Daddy," he said with almost a surprise in his voice.

"And why would your daddy ask you to read the label?"

"I don't know," Charlie finally said.

"I do," answered Russell and looked up at Charlie. "It was because your daddy could not read."

Russell waited for the impact of this statement to sink in.

"I'll leave you to think about this for a few days. I can teach you how to read. And I would consider it an honor to do so." Russell said as he started to put his books and papers back into his bag.

"People would laugh at me, being this old and just learning how to read," Charlie argued.

"Nobody would know, I wouldn't tell anybody. I'll come back in a few days and get your answer then," said Russell getting up.

"No," said Charlie stopping him. "I don't want to end up like my daddy. I'll learn if you think you can teach me."

"We'll start tomorrow morning then," said Russell, and they shook on it before he left the office.

Charlie took to reading like fish took the bait that Pops recommended. It wasn't long before he had mastered the simple books and was working on harder ones. Some days they had their lesson in Russell's boat with fishing rods in their hands. It was a red-letter day for Russell when he walked in the office and caught Charlie reading a seven-year-old boating magazine that had been sitting for so long on his couch.

CHAPTER SEVEN

Dave soon made it a habit of coming over every Wednesday night for roast and potatoes. Liria was getting used to having a policeman join them for dinner. She gradually recovered from her fear of being hauled off to jail, even though they reassured her she has done nothing wrong. Still, her fear made Russell worry that there might be something else that she was hiding.

This last Wednesday though, as Russell walked Dave out to his car, Dave turned and speaking softly said, "They picked up Liria's nephew."

"Will they ask Liria to testify?"

"We won't know that for weeks or maybe months. Do you think she could, or would it be too hard on her?"

"I think we better try to keep her out of the witness stand. She might end up saying too much." Russell said thoughtfully.

"What makes you say that? Has she dropped any hints of more things that are buried in the backyard?"

"No, maybe it's just my imagination but I think that there are a few more secrets about this house that she hasn't let on yet." Russell shook his hand and walked back to the house.

That evening he got an e-mail inviting him to be a speaker at a mission conference in Chicago. They apologized it was last minute but one of their speakers had become ill and couldn't make it. It was a group that he'd worked with before, and many of his friends would probably be there.

Then too it would be a break from the house. Lately, the job of getting this place into shape was looming larger and larger. Russell figured it would be good therapy to stay in a four-star hotel on the waterfront in Chicago. He quickly replied "yes" and then settled in to study what they wanted him to speak about.

The invite also jolted Russell back into the world that he had only recently retired from. He had been used to acclimating to new cultures and was surprised to find that he had adapted considerably to Ferndale. Pulling his mind away from this small town would be good for him.

Liria's response to his trip plan was telling.

"Have you heard anything about my sister from your friends in Albania?" she asked.

"No, but if I run into anybody at the conference I will be sure to ask again."

Sunday night Russell drove to Chicago. He returned the following Saturday well-rested, well-fed, and reconnected to friends around the world.

Russell was quickly jerked back to Ferndale. He had helped Liria open up a bank account shortly before he left. What greeted him was going to change the known universe.

"Liria, your bank card has arrived," he said with trepidation.

"Read it to me." was her response.

This confused Russell until he realized she was thinking it was like a Christmas card. He walked over and place it on the table in front of her as she was drinking her tea.

"This is a bank card. It helps you get your money out of your account. And with it you can pay for things without handling cash."

She looked at him as though he were speaking Chinese.

What happened next took the better part of an hour. Russell explained how to use the card, what it did, where she had to sign and how well she had to protect it. Afterward, she held it out as though it might explode.

Russell went back to work in his office, getting caught up in the week's mail. He was deeply into a long e-mail when he felt somebody staring at the back of his neck.

"I can buy things with this?" asked Liria without waiting for him to say anything.

"Yes."

"I can go to a restaurant and buy food?"

"Yes," he had previously explained to her the process of going to a restaurant and tipping.

"Let's go," she said as she turned to grab her purse.

"Liria, have you ever been shopping?"

"Well for sure! You know I have been to the grocery store and the five and dime on Main Street."

"But have you ever been to a large shopping center?"

"No, I could get all that I need here and I could not get there on my own. Besides I've never had enough money to just go shopping, so let's go." Liria said.

"I'll be there in a minute I need to finish this e-mail."

Liria did not respond verbally, but her body language clearly told him that after waiting for sixty-some years to go shopping like this, two more minutes would be a terrible inconvenience.

He took her to Wal-Mart and dropped her off. Thinking back it might not have been the best idea. Two hours later he came back to pick her up. She had one small bag and a big smile. At that point, he realized he'd never really seen her smile, at least not in the way she was smiling now.

"I bought you something." she handing him a Mars bar.

Smiling he asked, "How did it go?"

"At first I was very scared. All those people, all those lights. I almost walked out, but then I met Harry. He greeted me warmly and gave me a shopping cart. He has two children but they don't live near here. His oldest daughter has two sons and they all come over and visit every summer but usually they just e-mail and Facebook."

Russell realized that Liria had met and gotten to know the life story of a greeter at Wal-Mart. A man whom he himself had no doubt seen several times but never thought of actually talking to.

"Harry helped me find my way around. He pointed out the different departments. Whenever I got lost I could always find Harry and he could help me find what I was looking for. Such a nice man."

She buckled her seatbelt and settled in for the ride home. "Well at first I started putting things in my cart. There were a new color television and an alarm clock that had a radio on it. I found a new watch with what looked like diamonds around the face. I tried on several dresses and a new jacket. Up and down the aisles I went and my cart was getting fuller and fuller. It was almost like a game, to see if I could find one thing to buy from every row. Very quickly my cart was beginning to get full. I noticed some people watching me. It started to make me mad. This was my money and I could afford everything. I had gone years without buying anything because I had no money. So I put more things in my cart."

Liria looked out the window. Russell waited for her tell her story in her time.

"By the time I got to the grocery aisle, I thought I would need two carts. But then something strange happened. I did not like myself anymore. I thought, "Who is this person pushing all this stuff? Is she really happy with all the things that she has in the cart? I stopped in the middle of the aisle. Then I went back and started putting everything back on the shelves I had gotten them from. I was hungry so I went to the café and got a sandwich. There was an old lady there, drinking coffee. She looked hungry, so I bought her a sandwich too. She thanked me and smiled.

"After I had finished eating I thought I would like a candy bar. Then I thought about the old lady and how she smiled at my sandwich and how maybe she would want a candy bar too.

So I pushed my cart to the candy aisle of the store and there I got an idea."

Russell saw the smile come back to Liria's face.

"I thought maybe you would like a candy bar. Then I thought that maybe everybody would like a candy bar. So I bought five boxes of Mars bars. There must have been over hundred candy bars! When I went to pay I think they thought I was crazy. They asked me what I was going to do with all those candy bars. How many children did I have, was I a teacher, things like that. I simply told them that I was going to stand at the door and as people left the store I was going to give them a candy bar. They didn't believe me. Harry believed me. He helped me open up the boxes. Such a nice man. He had a small pocket knife."

Liria started talking with her hands as she went on with the story. "You know what is surprising? It wasn't easy. Giving away candy bars is not easy. Some people thought I was trying to sell them, others thought I was trying to raise money for a charity and they gave me coins but I gave them back. I explained to people I just wanted to help bring smiles to people's faces. The children understood and many of them gave me hugs. Once the word got out it was wonderful. The old woman from the café got one and told me she had not had a candy bar in over twenty years. Twenty years! Imagine that!"

Liria was animated by now. "Well, soon a man came out and asked me what I was doing. He said he was the manager of the store. He had heard that there was a riot. No, no riot, just a little old lady trying to make people happy. He asked me how many boxes of candy bars I had gone through. He noticed all the people around him smiling and eating chocolate. Then you know what he did? He went back into the store and brought out five more boxes of candy bars. It was a good thing to because I had run out and I forgot to save you one.

"Almost too quickly those were gone too. But I was left with many friends and happy memories, I can still see all those people's smiles. So much better than a new color TV."

Russell let her be quiet for a minute before he asked, "What's in the box?"

"I remembered that I could use a new pair of shoes." She reached into the bag and pulled out some tennis shoes. "Harry recommended them. He says he's on his feet all day and they don't hurt his feet like other shoes. He's such a nice man."

CHAPTER EIGHT

"So what did you learn in church today?" asked Liria as she placed a plate of lunch in front of him.

"I learned that the preacher is a heretic," replied Russell as he slumped into the chair.

He had been living in Ferndale for several months now, trying out different churches, looking for one that he could call home. Some Sundays he even just stayed home. The first church he visited was on its last legs, with only a few people left in the congregation. The next was too legalistic and only taught doctrine. The pastor of the church he had visited this morning turned out to be a heretic. That left a Haitian church where the service was in Creole.

"The man said you don't need Jesus to get to heaven!" he said.

Russell was used to working inter-denominationally as a missionary. It seemed that on the mission field denominations added color and flavor to a united church. Here they were dividing and built walls.

Liria crossed herself to protect her soul from these evil words.

"This is why I stopped going. Even the Catholic priest that would come once a month was doing bad things," exclaimed Liria, then quickly added, "But I still believe in God, I still pray and I watch church on television."

"Which church?" Russell was curious.

"Reverend Billy Graham."

"Good choice."

Russell was out of choices though, other than driving over an hour to get to another town, he was going to be churchless. Well, God would help him find a church. This was his prayer early Monday morning during his devotions. Within a few hours, God answered by having a church find him.

An old sedan pulled into the driveway and a Hispanic looking gentleman stepped out.

"Mr. Green? My name is Pastor Rivera," he said in an accented voice.

"Call me Russell." he said as he shook his hand.

"Call me Manuel."

"What can I do for you, Manuel?" Asked Russell as they sat down at the kitchen table.

"Well, I will get to the point, we have a small church that has been meeting at my house. Most of the people are Hispanic but our services are in English with some singing in Spanish. We can no longer fit in my living room and the neighbors are complaining. The police even came yesterday just as we were finishing up our service and told us we could not worship there anymore; something about zoning laws. The Chief of Police, however, gave me your name and number and said that you might have room for us to meet in your hotel here. I thought it best that I came over myself and see it with my own eyes, and for us to meet each other face-to-face."

By this time Liria had served them both tea.

"Well grab your cup and follow me. Take a look at what we have. I'm hoping to open this up as a guesthouse again but I have this big front room." Russell led the way into what had been the living and dining room area of the hotel. "There's not going to be much room for a band and I don't really have the system to support a lot of electronics, what do you think?"

The room had windows along one wall that looked out onto the front porch. On the opposite side, there were three doors that lead into side rooms. In the back, there was a small room and on the wall next to the kitchen was an old piano. All in all, the room was about sixteen feet wide and close to forty feet long.

"Well, we don't have a band, we have a man with an acoustic guitar and his daughter with a tambourine. If the piano works we might be able to find somebody to play that." Manuel walked over to the piano and cautiously tapped a few keys. There was a dull "plunk" sound.

"I'll see if I can find somebody to work on that." Russell noted, then looking at the room again, "I think you could probably get fifty people in here if you had the chairs. With a little rearranging maybe we could squeeze in seventy-five, what do you think?"

"We can supply the chairs, but would there be a place to store them here during the week?" asked Manuel.

"This room in the back might make a good storage room for you," Russell said, strolling over and opening it. "Whatever you can fit in here could store between Sundays. I would get you a key."

They both walked around the large room pacing out where they would put the rows of chairs and aisles. Finally, Russell motion for him to sit down on a couch.

"Physically I think you can do it, I wouldn't charge much for the use; it would be nice to have people over. I don't think we will get the guesthouse running in the next few months and even after that, there shouldn't be a problem in you holding church services here. But I do have some very important questions for you. I've been a missionary practically all my life and I'm quite fond of the word of God. I want to know what you would be preaching in my house." said Russell seriously.

"I only have a Bible school degree, so I only teach from the Bible. I don't know much about theology and church doctrine; the church I study is in the book of Acts. Our position as a church is that if it is in the Bible it's good. We have some people who speak in tongues and some who don't, we believe in healing and miracles and telling other people about Jesus.

We did not break off from any church, we started because a group of us were hungry for a church community. Most of the people who come are new believers. Naturally, we have some misfits that don't belong anywhere else. We don't even have a name for us as a church, we never felt the need for one yet."

They talked for quite a while about different points of Scripture until Russell was satisfied.

"Well you could start this Sunday but the place needs a little bit of cleaning," said Russell.

"We could have a few people come over on Saturday to clean and get ready if that would be alright." offered Manuel.

"Just not too early. Let's start at about nine, okay?"

"Great, we will see you on Saturday then." With that Manuel got up to leave.

"Lunch is ready, gentlemen," said Liria as she came into the room.

"You can't leave now, you must stay and have something to eat," said Russell and ushered him into the kitchen.

It was a delightful lunch. Liria had baked her famous byrek with a few other Albanian side dishes. Manuel ate with great pleasure.

As Manuel got into his car, Liria commented that he was the first Mexican to like her food.

"I don't think he's Mexican. I think he mentioned Spain," said Russell thoughtfully.

"I don't think he's Spanish," said Liria as she turned to do the dishes.

Russell got his flashlight and went to the piano. He wanted to see what made that interesting sound when Manuel hit the keys. It was dusty beyond belief and cobwebs were everywhere. Reaching in beyond where his flashlight could he felt around and found a nail that had been rusted off. Just below, resting against the strings was a key ring with a solitary key on it. Extracting and pocketing this, he gave the piano a thorough search but found nothing else but dust. He cleaned it the best he could, then called for a piano tuner.

That Saturday a crew of five showed up at nine o'clock prompt. They moved the couches and tables to the porch. Then the floor was mopped and scrubbed and the windows cleaned. Every wall and corner was dusted and wiped. The old closet was emptied and most of the stuff was thrown out. The newly tuned piano was wheeled across the room and set with its back against the closet. Then, after a lunch of sandwiches, a pickup truck pulled in with fifty brand-new plastic lawn chairs. It took the better part of an hour to get them arranged so that everybody was happy. Then some of the better comfortable chairs and couches were brought back in, having been dusted and cleaned. Two of the dining room tables were set against the wall next to the kitchen. When all was ready for the next day, Liria served coffee and tea. A thankful team left with cheerful goodbyes.

"So we are going to have church here," Liria stated. "This should be interesting."

"Looks that way." Russell suddenly remembered the key from the piano and fished in his pocket. "Have you ever seen this key or know what it's for?" he asked, holding it up.

"No, I've never used any keys around here, Tody always kept them. I've never had the need for keys."

Russell slipped the key onto his own key ring and tried to forget about it.

Church blessed Russell. He sat in the back and felt God's Presence in worship. He was touched by the level of community and fellowship. Manuel preached on Jonah, one of Russell's favorite passages, and brought out a few things that he had not thought of before. And he preached as if he knew more than just what a Bible school education could teach him.

After the service was over, Liria surprised them all by bringing out coffee and tea, with mugs, followed with some crackers and cookies. She then brought out a tray of glasses and a pitcher of lemonade. Russell was enjoying the conversations in both English and Spanish. People were having great fellowship together. Russell noticed that Manuel had grabbed a glass and filled it with hot tea. After a few minutes, he seemed to notice his mistake and poured the tea from the glass into a mug and continued drinking.

As people were leaving Russell thanked Manuel for the great sermon and added, "Can you come over tomorrow morning? I have a few ideas I'd like to run by you." They set an appointment for nine.

"I like our church," said Liria when everyone had gone, "they even helped with the dishes."

"Thank you for the refreshments, you didn't have to do that," Russell responded.

"Well, we don't get much company. You need to treat them right or they don't come back."

"What do you think of Pastor Rivera?"

"I like him," was all Liria said.

Russell liked him too, but there were a few things that didn't add up in his mind. Monday morning he was going to take a gamble. He was hoping that even though Manuel was not the man he said he was, that he would be the kind of man Russell thought he was, or Russell was going to lose a friend.

Monday morning, Russell was at his desk when Manuel walked in. In a casual voice, without lifting his head from what he was reading, Russell said, "Salaam-Alaikum" and without thinking, Manuel started to reply, "Alai......." Then his face turned white.

"Don't worry, your secret is safe with me. Come in and shut the door."

Manuel just stood there, not knowing if he could trust this man or not.

Russell stood up, "I'm sorry I shocked you, I didn't know you would react like this. I am a Christian, Jesus Christ is Lord, you're safe, please have a seat."

Manuel cautiously sat down. "How did you know? Who told you? How many others know?" he stammered.

"As far as I know, only me, and I only just guessed."

"Good guess, how did you figure out?"

"A few clues: you liked Liria's byrek, you drank tea from a glass and you preached about Nineveh like you used to live there, even calling it Mosul."

"I did; it's my hometown." Manuel relaxed a bit. He was shocked by the fact that somebody had figured him out, but at the same time relieved that he finally had somebody he could talk to about it. Russell let him be quiet, not pressing him for information until he was ready to give it.

"I feel as though I need to tell you the whole story. If I don't you may not understand how important it is that nobody else knows that I'm not really Manuel Rivera. Legally I am.

Legally that is my name now. But if I tell you, I need for you to promise not to tell anyone else."

"You have my promise." said Russell.

"If you break that promise, I could die a horrible death."

CHAPTER NINE

"My name is Mohammed, or at least it was," he began, "and I was born in Mosul, Iraq. My father became a Christian as a young man. He met my mother at a house church. They could not tell their parents, or they would have been killed.

"After they were married they started their own church in their own apartment. At most five or six people would come, and they would sit around drinking tea as if they were just having a polite gathering. This is how I grew up. Loving Jesus with all my heart, but being very secretive about it and telling no one."

Manuel leaned back in his chair and settled into the story.

"We would move every few years or when the group got too big. My father would place another man in charge and we would go to another part of town and start a new church. He must've started at least a dozen churches while I was growing up.

"I was about sixteen when we got word that they were coming for us. We had an agreed-upon password, a phrase that when we heard it we knew we had to leave. I do not know who delivered the news to my father, we had never seen him before, but we took it seriously and fled with just one change of clothing and our documents."

Manuel leaned forward. The tension of reliving this experience was evident on his face.

"We walked at night and hid by day. It was only through a miracle that we were able to make it across the border. We walked into Turkey. We had some money with us so we took a bus to Istanbul. When we got there the stories we heard from other refugees did not encourage us at all. Some had been waiting for asylum for fourteen years. Refugees were not allowed to work. Many of the women had been lied to and sold into prostitution to feed their children. Others told us stories of people being smuggled to Greece by boat only to be thrown into the water yards from shore and told to swim. Most refugees do not know how to swim.

"We decided to move on as fast as possible. We went through Bulgaria, crossing the border by bus at night. We dressed in our best clothes, so as to not look like refugees. We asked for a temporary visa, saying we were visiting relatives. We had addresses of churches in some countries and others we just made up. Father also had to bribe the officials several times. At every border, they didn't want us in and the old country didn't want us back. We had to keep on promising that we were only passing through."

Manuel had closed his eyes by now and was talking slowly, reliving the details.

"What helped was a letter from my father's brother in Spain. He had a company there. He was a legal resident and had been there for many years. The letter said that we were welcome to come and that he would care for us. The letter promised that he had enough money so that we would not be a burden to the government. This letter was written by my father after he carefully erased his brother's original letter.

"But the letter worked. It had an address and a signature and most of the countries we went through did not look at it long enough to realize it was very poor Spanish.

"At the Spanish border, they wanted to send us back to Iraq. I thought it was all over. All the weeks of traveling would be useless if we were sent back."

Manuel stood up now, pacing as he talked.

"We were all praying so hard. When they saw that we were in a circle they asked if we were Christians. We assured them we were and that we would be killed for it if we had to go back. Well, they went into the next room and talked quite a bit. We prayed even more. When they came out they said they had room for one more Christian family in Spain. After that, there were a lot of papers to fill out but we were in.

"My uncle was told of our arrival, but we did not go to his house. He was still Muslim. He would be honor-bound to try to kill us."

Manuel glanced over at Russell, checking to see if he was following. Satisfied, he went on.

"We went to Madrid at first. We looked until we found an evangelical church that would help us. With their help, we rented an apartment and started to learn Spanish. We threw away the clothes that we had. We did not want anybody to recognize us by what we wore. My father cut his beard. I had never seen him without a beard; it was a shock to me at first. My mother and my sister started to wear makeup, not to appear modern but as a disguise. My brother and I let our hair grow and I started to wear glasses. A picture of our family a year before would look nothing like a picture of us at that time. That is what we're trying to do because we knew that my uncle would be looking for us."

He took a deep breath as if trying to let go of the memory of that time.

"After about three months we could all converse in Spanish quite well, so we moved to a new city, not even telling our friends where we were going. My brother and I both got part-time jobs and started calling each other Manuel and Samuel. My father never left the house until long after dark but my brother and I were in school and had after school jobs.

"One night my brother told the family he thought he was being followed. He was sure that they did not follow them to our house but he felt quite convinced that somebody knew who he was at work. Because he was over eighteen my father thought the best idea would be that he would leave independently. We decided he should try and go to England."

Manuel leaned forward and covered his eyes with one hand.

"That night was the last time I ever saw my brother. If he got to England or not I do not know. We moved again shortly after that, but my sister stayed behind. She stayed with a family from the church. She was engaged to a young man there. Her last name is now Rios. She has three children and sends me letters once or twice a year but I have not seen her since.

"Later that year my father was killed. It was a hit-and-run. He was crossing the street when a car without lights ran over him, twice. We knew it was an honor killing but the police called it an accident."

Manuel was silent for a moment, then gathered the courage to go on.

"My mother and I moved back to Madrid, thinking we could hide better in a larger city. We went back to the church we had attended at first. After some years, my mother met and married an older man from the church and became Mrs. Rivera. I took the opportunity to claim that name as my own. I applied to and was accepted at a Bible School in Chicago. With my stepfather's help, I was able to provide documents to show that I was from Spain and my name was Manuel Rivera. It took a few more years but I eventually became a citizen of the United States. I have been pastoring churches and doing odd jobs since graduation. When the chance to come here opened up, I jumped at the opportunity thinking that a small town like this would be a very safe place."

He leaned forward and used his hands to emphasize what he was saying.

"So Mr. Green, my church, my friends, and even the United States government does not know who I really am. Only my mother, my sister and you do. I'm not afraid of the family back in Iraq finding me here, but if the government finds out that I am not who I said I was, maybe they would send me back to Iraq and there I would be found out as a Christian who left Islam."

Russell was quiet for a few minutes letting the story sink in. "So of course you have never married."

"Of course not," said Manuel, "in a marriage, you have to be open and honest about everything and I could not be honest about who I was."

"I give you my promise, no one will hear of this story from me," said Russell.

"I believe you, and I'm glad that you know now. I've needed a friend for many years but I've always had to be on guard. Now that you know I can relax around you. I've needed to tell my story to someone, perhaps even just to remind me of who I was and where I've come from. I often wonder about all the churches my father started in Iraq. I wonder how many Believers there are now, and how many people that my father brought to Christ have suffered for their faith as we have."

"I have missionary friends in Spain and England, maybe they could help find your brother."

"I don't know if I want to run the risk for him or myself of doing that. I know I will see him again in heaven, and I'm not the first one to give up family members for the sake of the kingdom of God."

"No you're not," replied Russell, "and I know many people with stories similar to yours. Perhaps I'll get a chance to introduce you to them. But if you ever want me to ask around to try and find your brother, just let me know."

"Maybe someday," said Manuel.

"Now, if I know Liria, she has some tea ready, but maybe you would prefer some Turkish coffee?"

"You mean real coffee?"

"I do indeed," said Russell with a smile.

CHAPTER TEN

"Hey, I hear you have a church meeting at your place," said Dave as Russell walked into Betty's a few days later.

"Yes, thanks to you. You ought to come and join us some Sunday," replied Russell.

"I can't. Didn't you know that the world would come to an end if I wasn't at the early mass every Sunday? At least that's what Father Paul tells me."

"Well then please don't, I like to enjoy a few more years of my retirement."

"You seem awfully busy for being retired."

Russell sighed, "And it's going to get worse. Who do I see about a building permit?"

"You mean your house is too small? I thought that place had about eight bedrooms."

"It's ten, and I just need to remodel. There's only one bathroom upstairs and I'd like to add a few more. I got a call from a friend of mine and he is sending a team of young people to help for two weeks, starting Monday."

"In the basement at City Hall, ask to speak to Sam. If Sam is not around, go back later. Under no circumstance should you talk to Harry. He is a good man but he will work extra hard to find more regulations for you to follow than what's necessary. He's new on the job and wants to impress people by how many hoops he can make folks jump through," said Dave.

With this new information, Russell headed to City Hall, his plans and drawings in tow. He had been working on this project for weeks now and when his friend called, saying that there was a work team available, he kicked into high gear. He didn't know how much work they could get done but he had to have the master plan drawn out. He went over the layout again in his mind.

With the downstairs meeting room now being used as a church, he didn't want to change that too much. Liria had taken over Tody's office. It had become a pantry that doubled as a television room where Liria liked to watch her soap operas in the morning. Flowery curtains hung at the window and he had given everything a new coat of paint last month. A comfortable chair was brought in facing the small color television sitting on the shelf next to boxes of oatmeal, bags of flour and extra dishes. Liria's bedroom was next door and, as far as he knew, didn't need anything. He had never seen inside it.

Beyond that was the small room he used as an office. He had cut a doorway between his office and his bedroom which came next in line. Then came the stairs. Along the front of the house, there was the porch then the main room. At the back of this, across from the stairs, was the storage room/office that he had turned over to Manuel to use for his church. Now that the church was meeting in his house he would like to put in a second bathroom on the main floor but couldn't quite figure out where to squeeze it in. He would have to work on that later.

Upstairs it was simpler. Eight rooms, four on each side, with a single bathroom sticking out over the space where the kitchen porch was down below. His plan was simple. He would turn the two middle bedrooms on the backside of the house into four bathrooms. This would give the two rooms on the backside private bathrooms, while the four rooms on the front side of the house would share the other two. He wasn't quite sure what to do with the existing bathroom. He wasn't even sure it worked.

When he reached City Hall he gathered up his papers and walked downstairs to the planning commission office. He knew he was in the right place when he smelled ink and carbon paper. As he went in, a rather large lady with an enormous amount of gray hair piled on top of her head was just handing a package to a young man.

"Hi, I'm looking for Sam? I need a building permit," said Russell tentatively.

"I can help you with that," said the young man setting down his package.

"No Harry," said the lady, "you need to get those documents up to records and don't come back until you see them filed correctly, then you better take your break. I can handle this man."

Harry seemed disappointed as he picked up his package of files and headed up the stairs.

Waiting until the door was closed the lady introduced herself. "I'm Samantha, but most folks just call me Sam. Dave gave me a call and told me you were on the way. Those files that I gave Harry will keep him busy for at least an hour. Now, what can I do for you?"

Silently thanking God for a friend like Dave, Russell spread the plans out on the table and went over the details of what he was planning on doing with his house.

"Well, if you're going to operate a hotel that falls under a whole different kettle of fish. There's a whole new set of hoops and regulations you have to jump through. All the changes you're going to have to make happen with that old place ain't going to make it an easy walk in the park. I hope you got a lot of money to burn so you can grease the bureaucratic wheels. And even with a full house you probably won't see diddly squat of profit for a few years. I think you would be a dodo bird to try, but if you're mule-headed enough, I'll get started on the mountain of paperwork." Sam eased herself out of her chair and headed to the file cabinet. "So just how much are you planning on charging for what are your fancy rooms?"

"Nothing."

"Nothing?"

"I'm not going to operate as a hotel. I have lots of friends that fly back and forth and I want to offer them a room for a few days. I'm not going to charge anything."

"If you're not charging anything you're not a hotel," said Sam with her hands on her hips.

"I guess not."

"And the way I see it, you're just remodeling your own house, not opening it up for business." Sam walked back to the table. She reached up to her hair and fumbled around in the pile for a while and pulled out a ballpoint pen. Frowning, she shoved it back in and fumbled a few moments more before pulling out a pencil. She made some marks on his plans.

"Make sure these two bathrooms have exhaust fans, put everything on a GFI circuit, a separate one for each bathroom and update your smoke detectors. That's about it." She reached below the table and pulled out two pieces of paper. Replacing the pencil and pulling out the pen she scribbled a few notes on each and handed the pen to Russell. "Sign here, and place this one in the window in the front of your house. That'll be forty dollars."

Russell thanked her profusely and gladly paid the money. He gathered up the paperwork and his plans and headed to the hardware store.

He'd started making a list of what he needed weeks ago and ended up with a three-ring binder with different tabbed sections for electrical, plumbing, paint and building supplies. Whenever he saw a sale advertised at any lumberyard in driving distance, he stocked up. He also was a frequent visitor to any yard sale in town. He now had enough material stored in his barn to get started.

"Where have you been all morning?" asked Pop when Russell walked into the hardware store.

"I didn't know you were expecting me," said Russell, a little surprised.

"Well, our sale started yesterday and I haven't seen you yet. You've become quite predictable."

"I was busy trying to get my building permit."

"Did you deal with Sam?"

"Yes, she's a really interesting character."

"What did she pull out of her hair today?"

"Just a pen and pencil, why, what else does she keep up there?"

"I've seen her pull out a stapler. Rumor has it that's where she keeps her lunch."

Not enjoying the mental picture, Russell tried to change the subject. "I need some of that electrical tape."

"Sold out."

"Sold out? Hmmm, I'm going to need some on Monday I've got a whole team coming and there's a lot of rewiring to do."

"Yup, sold out except for this box I've been keeping behind the counter for you," Pop smiled as he placed the box on the counter.

"Thanks, how did you know I needed electrical tape?"

"Easy. You haven't bought any yet! It's something you always need when you remodel and there hasn't been a sale anywhere around here on it the last few months."

"Brilliant reasoning," said Russell.

"That's how I stay in business," smiled Pop.

Russell paid for the whole box and headed home for lunch.

Over his food, Russell went over the menu plans for the next two weeks with Liria. Being from America, he figured these young people would not want the Albanian cooking that he had gotten used to. Recipes for macaroni and cheese, chicken and rice, spaghetti and pizza were brought out and gone over. This afternoon he would drive his pickup to the grocery store. This was going to put Liria to the test. He wasn't quite sure how his housekeeper was going to handle a bunch of Christian young people. They were not the clientele that she had been used to.

Monday morning at ten o'clock his porch was filled with suitcases and backpacks. The school bus parked in the yard. The six people to whom they belonged were gathered around the kitchen table enjoying Liria's coffee cake while drinking coffee, tea, and colas.

The oldest in the team was their leader, a young man in his thirties named Tim. The youngest was a redheaded from Scotland named Fergus. The only other man on the team was a studious looking chap that went by several names, but whose official name was Robert. The other three members of the team were sisters from the mid-west farming country. Breanne, Casey, and Marybeth. It took Russell a week before he could tell them apart.

With the two-week schedule laid out before them, they first choose two people to help with each meal. One would help prepare and one help clean up. With that finished, they addressed the daily agenda. Breakfast would be at 9:00 a.m. after people had their private devotions, lunch at 12:30 p.m., supper at 6:30 p.m. and Russell would have an evening devotion right after supper.

They planned a trip to the beach halfway through the two weeks, but first things first. Everybody was assigned rooms and brooms and got busy. Before they slept tonight, mattresses would have to be aired out, rooms swept and mopped, windows washed and curtains hung.

Russell's idea was that everyone would take one room and clean it themselves. Marybeth, however, took over laundry chores and while she was doing that Casey swept the room for her. Tim and Robert made a team hanging the curtains. Breanne cleaned out Fergus' room while Fergus single-handedly dragged all the mattresses to the backyard beat them soundly and set them to air leaning against the clotheslines.

Having finished a good chunk of the work, they enjoyed macaroni and cheese for lunch, not knowing that it was the first such dish Liria had ever made.

Robert became the window cleaning expert that afternoon. Tim attacked the mop like he was wrestling with a bear. As each room became ready, Fergus hauled up a mattress and Meredith and Casey made the beds like a professional house cleaning team. When they were done the whole place smelled clean, for the first time in years.

During supper, Liria disappeared for a few minutes. She went upstairs to inspect their work and when she came down she had a big smile on her face.

As they were relaxing after dessert, Russell got out his Bible and talked about Jonah.

"Nineveh was the last place that Jonah wanted to go. Preaching to his enemies was the last thing he wanted to do. Even though he had great success preaching to them, Jonah wasn't happy and neither was God. God was out to do more than save the people in Nineveh; he was after Jonah's heart. The last part of the book is not about saved people, but God sharing his heart for the lost with Jonah."

Russell paused to let this sink in a bit.

"Before you do anything for missions, make sure your heart is after the things that are on God's heart. If not, beware of big fish."

Russell said a quick prayer and sent them off thinking they would get to bed soon. He'd forgotten what age his guests were. Tables were quickly pushed together and chairs were brought around. Board and card games came out, along with music. Fergus went into the kitchen and came out with bottles of soda and boxes of cookies. Russell went to bed.

Several hours later, when the young people finally went upstairs, they found that Liria had placed a Mars bar on each one of their pillows.

CHAPTER ELEVEN

The week had gone by quickly and work was progressing smoothly. The new bathrooms were almost all framed and drywalled in. The old wallpaper was quickly coming off in the bedrooms. The group had worked well together as a team, each filling in where needed.

Things had progressed so well that Russell had most of the team out digging up soil for a garden outside. There was just one wall left in the last room. It was when Breanne started to take the paper off that Russell noticed something unusual.

"This wall seems different," she said, "and look there's a hole underneath this piece."

Russell stooped to inspect the hole. He was used to holes in the walls and finding areas that needed plastering and patching, but it was the shape of this one that started his brain flip-flopping. It was a keyhole.

"Let me see if this can be patched, he said. Why don't you take a break and go help them in the garden? I can manage this last bit of paper after it's patched."

Russell stood there for a minute waiting until he heard her feet on the first floor and heading out the back door. He pulled the old key from the piano out of his pocket. His hand shook a little as he put the key in the hole and turned it. It unlocked.

It only took Russell a few seconds to clear away the rest of the wallpaper. The clear shape of a door emerged. It was about one foot by one foot. Then walking to the bedroom door he locked it from the inside. He went back to the door in the wall. He slowly opened the door in the wall. His mind was already guessing what was inside.

Since he had moved into this house he had had many surprises, not the least being his first meeting with Liria, but nothing compared to this. In a neat little cupboard built into the wall was a pile of cash.

He quickly closed the door to the safe and locked it. He took a deep breath. Already a jumble of thoughts were running through his mind. "This is not my money. Of course, this is my money; it's my house. I could buy that yacht. I'll have to share it with Liria. I don't have to share this with anybody."

He took a deep breath and shook his head to clear his thoughts.

"Russell," he said to himself, "you've never been a greedy man and you are not going to start now!" He left the room and was locking it from the outside when Liria started shouting.

"Mr. Green, Mr. Green, the children, what are they doing in the garden?"

Although most of the young people were adults by age, Liria still referred to them as children. When Russell caught up to her he tried to calm her down.

"They are just expanding the garden."

"But they can't!"

"Why not? As long as we have the manpower we might as well turn the soil over even if we don't plant until the spring."

"But where they are digging, they shouldn't. William is under there."

Russell flew out the door. He hoped his shaking was not noticeable when he redirected the garden expansion to the other side.

Another body in the ground was not what he needed right now. Now he needed a few minutes of quiet personal time to deal with, how much was it? Millions? Could be, the stack was high enough. William would have to wait. He would ask Liria about him later when no one else was around.

When he got back into the house, Liria was noticeably calmer and drinking a cup of tea. She was obviously lost in memories.

"None of the men liked William. They used to call him, 'Billy the Kid', but I liked him. He was always nice to me."

"Some notorious gangster," thought Russell, "So bad that they named him after a famous bank robber. Bank robber? All that money upstairs...?" So was he now involved in a bank robbery? Surely the statute of limitations was long over by now and he would have no trouble keeping the money?

Russell's hand was almost on the suitcase when he was called out again. This time from the basement where the men were hooking up the drainpipes from the new bathrooms upstairs.

Tim was shining a flashlight at another hole in the wall. This one was just the size of the sledgehammer that Fergus was holding.

"I didn't mean to, I can fix it, I was just trying to kill a nasty spider." Said Fergus. "But I think you better look through that hole before I patch it."

Russell knelt down and using a flashlight he peeked through the hole. There was a whole other room complete with chairs, lights, a carpet on the floor and what looked like a still and a small printing press. He noticed a set of stairs going up along the back wall. Guessing how far they were from the wall he went upstairs and paced off the distance. It came to the closet in his room.

Pulling back the carpet on the floor of his closet he noticed the trapdoor. The boys were with him, curious as to what he was up to. Russell was not sure if he wanted witnesses. But he didn't know how to tell them to leave.

The trapdoor opened with a squeak and armed with flashlights they creaked down the stairs brushing away cobwebs as they went.

Their eyes were getting used to the dim light when suddenly the room was ablaze.

"I found the light switch," said Tim.

Blinking in the brightness they found themselves in what definitely was the 1920's version of a man cave.

Fergus headed over to the still and eyed it with admiration. Tim promptly sat down in the overstuffed chair and kicked his feet up on the ottoman. Robert headed to the printing press.

"My grandfather had one very similar to this. Sadly, this is too old and broken to be used again. It looks like it was well used, though, they could have made gallons and gallons of whiskey with this." said Fergus.

Robert spoke up, "This printing press could be made to run again, but it was only made to print one thing:" he turned and looked at Russell, "money."

Russell wished that the chair was empty and he could flop down into it. He was feeling the blood drain from his face. All in one day, a pile of cash, a dead bank robber laying in his garden and now an illegal still and a printing press for making counterfeit money.

Tim had his eyes closed and appeared to be sleeping but he opened one eye and asked, "I suppose we should probably call the police."

Russell had to think for a minute. Did he really want the police nosing around the place with a lot of cash upstairs and another dead body in the garden? Especially when the chief of police was a good friend of his. Would somebody go to jail? Would he get into trouble for any of this?

"No, I don't think so."

"What?" exclaimed the three boys.

Russell then realized that he had said what he thought out loud. "No, I mean yes," he corrected himself. "The Chief of Police is a friend of mine. Let's go up and call him."

The four of them thumped up the stairs.

"Hello, Dave, Russell here. I think you better come on over, we found something else." There was a pause. "I'd rather not describe it on the phone, but there is no emergency." Russell hung up.

The whole team was having coffee and tea when the Chief of Police drove in. They all remain seated as Russell took Dave over to the trapdoor.

"There is a whole room here that I did not know existed. I had thought it was just a partial basement but then we broke through a wall and found this whole space. I asked Liria about it but she had no idea either. I believe she's telling the truth." Russell explained as they headed down the stairs.

If Dave was surprised to find a still and a counterfeit printing press he did not show it. He took his time going over each item, sniffing bottles and moving levers.

Russell was glad the chair was empty. He patiently waited until Dave was done with his investigation. Dave held up the plates from the printing press and turned to talk to Russell. "Well, these plates are too old. They haven't printed money like this for a couple of decades. I'll take these with me now but I may want to come back for the whole press as evidence. This may clear up a couple of cold cases. I think however, I can prove that you had nothing to do with this." Dave chuckled. "You do however get into some very unusual circumstances. The still, however, is completely legal and you could crank out a few gallons for your personal consumption under current laws."

"I have it from reliable sources that this still is beyond repair. If Liria doesn't want it for sentimental reasons, I'm going to scrap it," replied Russell.

"Pity," said Dave, "it reminds me of the one my grandfather had."

As Dave was leaving, the boys showed the girls around the basement. Work for the day was pretty much over. Fergus explained the workings of the still to the three girls and Robert showed how the printing press ran. They spent the rest of the day looking through the room for mislaid counterfeit bills and hidden bottles of whiskey. Tim, however, spent his time with a pencil, pad of paper and a tape measure. When he was done they had a huddle to which Russell was not invited.

After his coffee on Saturday morning, Russell sent the team off in their bus for a day at the beach. Russell went to talk to Liria.

"Tell me more about the William that's in the garden," he asked her.

"Billy was nice to me, probably because of the food I gave him. But all the men hated him and said he was mean."

"Was that the men who killed him?"

"Oh no, he died of old age," she paused. "That's why we didn't eat him."

Bank robbers, stills, counterfeit printing presses, dead bodies and now cannibalism. Russell went numb for a few minutes as it all sunk in. Then as his brain began to work again, two words came to the forefront: kid and Billy.

"Liria, was William a goat?"

"Why of course he was my old Billy goat. What did you think he was?"

"I thought he was a bank robber. You see I found a safe in the upstairs bedroom filled with money and I guess my imagination took over. By the way, do you know anything about all the money that's in the safe upstairs?"

"So that's where he put it," said Liria slowly.

"Who?"

"The nice man from Romania. I had heard that he left a lot of money hidden here, but we never found it."

"Do you think he stole it?"

"Oh no, it was his money. He was a very wealthy man He said something about being in the government and when the Communists took over he had to leave."

Russell got up from the table and went upstairs. He brought the money down to his office desk. His eyes could tell him what he now suspected. It was not American money. It was millions and millions in old Romanian Lei. It was totally worthless.

It did have one value though. It made an amazing illustration for his Bible study that night on laying up treasures for yourself in heaven where moth and rust do not destroy.

On Monday they found a second use for it. It became the new wallpaper for the bedroom that it was found in.

CHAPTER TWELVE

Russell took great care to clean the paintbrush. He put the rollers and the paint tarps away in the basement. While down there he took a few minutes to stroll through the new door that had been put in the wall. The wall that he had thought was the end of his basement until Fergus put a hole in it and discovered the other room. At the initiative of the team, the room had been converted into a den.

The counterfeiting press was hauled off to the police station for their museum. The still had been converted into an amazing flower box complete with plastic flowers coming out of the tubes that used to produce bootleg whiskey. The walls were painted white, and the fresh smell still lingered. The floor was swept and cleaned with a secondhand carpet laid out. Along one wall stood an old console television and phonograph that had been repaired by Robert to include a jack for phones and MP3 players. The stairs that lead up to his closet had been redone and secured. A new closet space was in the process of being made under the stairs leading up to the top floor.

He was pleased with how the work had come together. It took him a week or two to finish up what the team didn't get to but now he felt ready to invite guests. In fact, he had been sending out e-mails to his friends explaining the house, its location, and his intentions. Replies had started coming in.

It was that time of year when many missionaries and international workers find themselves roaming about America speaking at churches and other gatherings. So he was not surprised to find several of his friends glad to take him up on his offer.

When the e-mails started to come in he made a trip to Wal-Mart to pick up a large desk calendar to keep track of who was coming when.

In amongst the e-mails was one from his friend in Albania. He had found Liria's sister.

"My friend found Bora." Russell paused to let this fact sink in. "She lives in your parent's house. We can arrange for you to speak with her."

Liria's face was blank. It seemed as though all the blood ran out of it.

Russell tried again.

"Liria, we found your sister. She is alive and well and living in your parent's house. If you want to talk to her we can call her tomorrow morning."

"No." Liria said as she jumped up from the table and ran out of the house letting the screen door slam behind her.

Russell waited until he could hear the steady squeaking of the rocking chair on the porch. He picked up Liria's teacup and went out to join her. Setting the cup on the table next to her chair he eased into the wicker chair on the other side and waited.

"She had become as dead to me," Liria began slowly, "It took many years for me to grieve the loss of my family. It was easier for me to imagine them all dead than to go on living so far away from them. I even gave up trying to remember my own language. For all my life I have never traveled outside this little town more than once or twice. I cannot even imagine what my hometown in Albania would look like now. Maybe it is better that I just leave it alone, I don't think my heart could take bringing that past up again."

Russell prayed silently. He got up and went to Liria's office and picked up a picture that was on the shelf. Coming back to the front porch he handed the picture to Liria. "Who is this a picture of?"

"Mr. Green, you know who that is."

"Yes, but I think it would be good for you to say it."

"That is me, it was taken just before I had to leave Gurdeti."

"Are you worried that the town you left still exists?" Russell paused but received no reply. "Are you afraid that the same people you left behind are still there?" Russell waited but still, Liria said nothing. Russell picked up the photograph he had brought out earlier. "You have changed a bit," he said with a gentle smile, "and just as much as you have changed, I bet they have all changed too."

It was a long while until Liria spoke. The only thing that moved around them were the tears that came down Liria's face.

"My sister was always the most beautiful one. Do you suppose she has gotten old and fat?"

"Do most women in your village get older and fat?"

"Yes, it seemed like it was the tradition."

"Then I would assume your sister is old and fat." With that Russell got up and went to his room, leaving Liria to work out the math that the same amount of time has passed in Albania as has passed in America. Perhaps her old fears had no basis.

Russell went back to work organizing what was rapidly becoming an international dinner party. Several friends were coming through around the same weekend. Everyone was to bring a dish from their own country or the one that they were working in. Altogether there would be more than one dozen nations represented in food. The thought of this almost got Russell's mind off from Liria's problem.

"Mr. Green, Mr. Green let's call her now!" interrupted Liria.

"We can't, it's the middle of the night there," replied Russell.

He turned and saw a blank look come across Liria's face. Remembering that she was basically unschooled he showed her his globe.

Early the next morning Russell set up the Skype appointment with an Internet café in Liria's hometown. For the most part, Russell left them alone but he occasionally walked to the kitchen and found Liria holding up different items to the camera to show her sister. If Liria had forgotten any of her language it all came back now. Russell knew a few common greetings and phrases, but it was all lost in the speed and confusion of two sisters talking again after so many years.

In the meantime, the date for the party was finally set. This meant Russell had two weeks to get a few more rooms ready. It would be good to see everybody again. Catching up would be interesting. A lot of water had gone under the bridge.

Some of the people coming were directors and leaders of mission organizations. They knew more about what was going on in the world than most news reporters. Russell almost felt distanced from the world in small-town Ferndale.

"What will we talk about?" he said absentmindedly.

He had more important things that needed his immediate attention. One of which was saying goodbye to her sister in the next room.

"How do you solve a problem like Liria?" he hummed the tune to himself. Here he had an older Albanian woman who might have to testify at a grand jury convicting her own nephew of mob-related activities.

"God, you are going to have to work another miracle here," prayed Russell as he walked back to the kitchen.

Russell could tell that Liria was bubbling with something she did not want to spill out quite yet. As soon as he closed off the Skype connection she exploded.

"She's fat!" Liria almost screamed, "She is so fat! And she actually looks older than me!" Liria was beaming brighter than Russell had ever seen her before. He watched as she danced around the kitchen.

"Thank you so much! Thank you so much, Mr. Green, you have healed a lot of old hurts and made my heart young again." She then leaned up and kissed him on the cheek.

Russell decided to leave her in her joy and went back to his office.

The next Saturday there was a similar call but without the extreme emotion, it was simply sisters catching up on three, almost four decades of memories and comparisons. The following Saturday the call to Albania was cut short when the guests started to arrive.

There were about thirty people that showed up. Some just came for the meal, some were spending the night, others pulled up in motorhomes. Some were his invites, others had invited their friends. There was a lot of coming and going. People pitched in where they saw a need. Leaders of organizations became bellhops, well-known preachers became dishwashers and cooks. Russell remembered handing the keys to his pickup truck to somebody he had not yet met, who was being sent to the grocery store to pick up some last-minute items.

"It will all work out," he thought. He had invited Dave too, but as of yet had not seen him. Dave did not show. The party got started at about five with hors d'oeuvres from three different countries. There were Chinese dim sum, Lebanese stuffed grape leaves, and Japanese gyoza. The main dishes tried to outdo each other. Each one was unique in flavor and presentation. The smells were incredible; the tastes were even better. They were just getting out the desserts when Russell noticed the Edsel pulling into his driveway.

"You are late," said Russell as he opened the door.

"And I'm not staying," replied Dave. "There was a bad accident on the main road. The man and his wife are pretty banged up and were taken to the hospital. The boy was in the backseat and was not hurt, but I don't think he understands anything that we ask him. He doesn't seem to speak English. I thought of your group here and wondered if maybe you can figure it out.

"Even if you can't I'm sure you have some people here that can help take care of him until we can find more family. Right now we have nothing to go on. The couple had no identification and no driver's license, and we are still trying to figure out if the car was registered or not. Anyways, your house is more comfortable than the police station for a young boy and probably has better food." With that, Dave turned and walked back to his car. It was going to be a long night for him.

The boy was soon the center of attention and as Russell explained the situation each one tried their language out on him. One by one languages got eliminated. Out went Spanish, French, German, Italian and even Chinese, although the boy did not look oriental. People began looking in their memories for other languages. Liria tried Albanian to no success. Farsi was tried, as was Welsh, but they were all striking out. Some even tried ancient Greek and Hebrew.

"Let's see what foods he likes, and get a clue from that," suggested Russell.

That didn't help, although he leaned towards Mediterranean foods. Like most eight-year-old boys he ate anything, and quite a bit of it.

Russell studied the child. He had a knit hat pulled down low over his ears that he refused to take off. His clothes definitely were not those of a refugee. He did not eat like he was famished or malnourished. Someone suggested that he just couldn't hear or speak, but that was soon proven false because he followed people's voices and his eyes followed noises around the room. As he was getting desert he started humming an interesting tune.

It was then Russell got an idea. Going into his office and returning with a yarmulke he sat down next to the boy and started the Shema.

"She-ma Israel....."

The boy looked up from his plate of food and completed the Shema with Russell. It was only then that the boy took off his hat and they notice the curly long hair hanging down in front of his ears.

"He can't be Jewish, we tried Hebrew," someone said.

"Not local Israeli, but Sephardic I believe," said Russell opening up his laptop.

In a minute he was on a Skype call to a friend in Turkey. "Mike, wake up your neighbor I need him to speak Ladino to someone here," he said.

It took a while for Russell to explain to his sleepy friend the importance of communication. After a while, another grumpy voice came on and said something that nobody else in the room understood except one small boy.

With multi-level translation, Mike's friend spoke with the boy, translated to Mike, who spoke with Russell. Gradually the story came out. Russell called Dave and explained it to him.

"They are from Turkey and are Sephardic Jews. It's a small minority. The boy was traveling with his aunt and uncle. The whole family is moving to America. They came early so the boy could get enrolled in school. His parents were coming the next day and they borrowed a car from a neighbor to go to the airport to pick them up. They couldn't get a hotel, so they were going to drive through the night. I've got all the details of their names, addresses, and the parent's flight numbers."

It was communicated back by the translator that his aunt and uncle were doing fine but would not be able to leave the hospital for a few days.

Dave assigned one of his deputies to find a social worker to take the boy to Chicago O'Hare Airport in the morning and collect his parents. Russell volunteered to go with them.

The party ended on a happy note. Someone picked up on the Skype idea and called a few other friends. Then they had a conference call, getting people from every time zone online.

When Russell returned the next day with the boy's parents he found a few guests still lingering. One was his friend from Albania that had helped to find Liria's sister.

After he had helped carry bags for the new guests into their room, he pulled Russell aside.

"Say, what are you doing at the end of next month? he asked.

"I've got to paint the side of the barn and trim my toenails. Why? Do you have something more interesting for me to do?"

"I need a main speaker for a conference in Albania." his friend let this sink in a minute. "It's in Tirana, I can cover your expenses but not much more. Are you interested?"

"How long do I have to think it over?"

"About one more minute. They are thinking of scrapping the whole conference because the main speaker can't make it. I told them that you would probably be available and they're jumping at the chance. Please say yes; it'll be like old times."

"Oh, I hope it will be better than that. I'll be there, just send me the details."

"Some of the info is on your desk, I'll send the rest in an email when I get back to the office tomorrow," his friend said as he got into his car and pulled away.

As Russell walked back into the house he prayed, "Oh Lord, this is a strange retirement to put me into. How many miracles can you work in one day?"

Then he corrected himself. "What a silly prayer."

CHAPTER THIRTEEN

Russell sat on the front porch drinking his second cup of coffee. Autumn was approaching. He enjoyed the leaves beginning to change color. The breeze was a bit cool. High flying wild geese gave hint of the approaching winter.

It was during those few moments of each day when he poured out his heart to God and waited for him to answer. It was a discipline he loved. Early in his missionary career, he had had to act and act fast. He had relied on his skill and knowledge. Then he had learned to seek God's heart and found he was being led.

Soon he would be flying to Albania. It was a country most people couldn't find on a map. To Russell, it seemed as natural as booking a two-week vacation in Florida.

He told his friend that he would handle buying his own ticket because he had a plan. Maybe he should say God had a plan. The details and possible outcomes started coming together in his mind as he finished his cuppa. There was only one date that he had to check on. He felt confident that it would fall within the two week period that he would be gone. He went back into the house, rinsed out his coffee cup and went to make a phone call.

"Hey, Dave, Russell here, any word on that court date for Liria's nephew?"

"Are you a psychic? It just came across my desk this morning. Let's see, yes, October 25th. That gives us just over a month to figure out what to do with Liria."

"I got it handled, or I should say God has a plan. I'll fill you in on it later, I've got to get some paperwork started." Russell hung up the phone, took a deep breath, and went into the kitchen. He had to be careful how he worded what he was going to say next.

"Liria? How would you like to go see your sister?"

Liria just stared at him as if he was speaking a foreign language.

"I have to fly to Albania. You could come with me and stay with your sister while I am at my conference."

Russell poured Liria a cup of tea. Tea was Liria's remedy for just about anything.

Without saying a word or even looking at him, Liria took several sips from the cup.

"You do not have to make up your mind right now. We have about a week before we should buy our tickets, but we should get started on your passport today." Russell made it a point not to stare at her or look like he was anticipating any form of a verbal answer. He made sure his pauses were long enough for Liria to process each sentence.

"We would need to get your birth certificate and citizenship papers together then head to the post office, preferably before lunch." He paused again, waiting a full minute. "If you decide not to go to Albania, a passport is a handy thing to have, it would not be a waste of time or money to get one." Russell then walked out of the room, leaving Liria to her thoughts.

He busied himself in his office for several minutes. He did a few preliminary searches for flights. He thought of all the fun places he could stopover on the way. It was almost a hobby of his to see what strange cities he could get a long layover in. "Not this time, better make it as direct as possible with Liria," he thought to himself.

About an hour later when he walked back into the kitchen he found Liria sitting at the table, with a stack of papers in front of her. When she turned her head to look at him he could not tell if she'd been crying or was joyful. Her whole face was full of emotions.

"Let's go, I'm ready," she said as she stood up.

Liria was quiet during the whole process of filling in the forms and getting her pictures taken. Talking only when necessary to answer questions, Russell had to convince her to have her process expedited. It was an additional expense she didn't want to pay. It was also long past lunchtime. So in an effort to appease Liria, Russell treated them to lunch at the local burger joint.

Liria kept her quiet countenance all during lunch. But upon getting back into the pickup truck, she turned to Russell and asked, "Does God answer all your prayers?"

Not wanting to start a theological debate, Russell chose to reply in a question. "Why do you ask?"

"This morning I woke up early and turned on the radio. There was a preacher and he was talking about how good God is. How God is a loving father and wants to give good gifts to his children. Well I started having a conversation with God, or maybe it was all just in my head, I asked God how good was He and how could He prove that he was good to me. He seemed to say, try me. So I told him that I wanted to go see my sister. I just finished praying when you came in." Liria paused. "So does God answer all your prayers like that?"

Russell laughed with relief. "Well, he certainly answered yours!"

When they got home Russell went to his office and started making a list. The enormity of the task ahead of him was not hidden to his multicultural, world traveling, adventure-seeking lifestyle. He had to prepare a sixty-something-year-old Albanian lady to fly halfway across the world.

He knew better than to dump a lot of new information on Liria all at once. Systematically he brought new ideas to her on a daily basis. He started by showing her pictures of the type of airplane that they would be flying on. He demonstrated with the kitchen chairs how close the seats were. He explained the size of the bathrooms and how they worked. He even tried on several occasions to explain time zone changes while in flight, how even though they would fly during the night, it would only last a few hours.

As time went by he was able to make her understand that even though she was born in Albania, she was an American citizen and would have to go through customs as an American.

As anticipated, the hardest part was food. The fact that she could not bring her own food onboard the plane was an illogical concept to her. She needed her thermos of tea, homemade yogurt in small Mason jars and her secret recipe applesauce. Russell assured her they would provide food onboard the plane and that even if she brought it, security would take it away.

"What?" She almost yelled in disbelief, "My food is illegal?" Nothing seemed more incredible than this to her.

Russell patiently explained to her that it wasn't her food but the general policy of security on an airplane. While he was doing it he himself saw the absurdity of such travel rules.

He had her start packing two weeks before the flight. He knew what she was thinking. Out came the steamer trunks that she had used so many years ago.

He surprised her with two brand-new lightweight suitcases. He was grateful that the airlines he chose and his frequent-flier miles allowed them two bags each.

It literally took days for her to grasp the concept of 50 pounds each. He had to remind her that she did not need a year's supply of toothpaste or soap.

He had her practice walking around the house with her suitcases and carry-on. In spite of the lessons that he gave her he had to confiscate several items. They set aside knitting needles, scissors and a jar of clear liquid that smelled like paint thinner.

"What's this?" he asked.

She hung her head a little sheepishly, "It's the last jar of homemade raki that my husband made. It's a traditional welcoming gift."

"We will have to find something else," Russell explained.

The last main hurdle was money. The bank card had been a recent addition to her life. Now he tried to explain that she could use the same card in Albania. Finally, she just accepted by faith that her money in America would show up in the bank machine in Albania.

Liria seemed to be in a state of shock. Russell wondered if he had given her too much information too soon or too much all at once.

They went over the schedule. It should work out fine. They would land at the airport in the capital and spend the first night at his friend's guesthouse. The next day they would take public transportation to Gurdeti. Russell would then spend most of that day with her, getting her set up and take the last bus back to the capital. He had about a week's worth of meetings, then wanted to take a few days to see some familiar sights. He would then make his way back to Gurdeti to pick up Liria. They would spend one night back in Tirana before their early morning flight back home. All in all, it would be about a two-week trip.

Russell felt that if everything went poorly with Liria she could at least handle two weeks. He even hinted to her that she could come back early to the capital. Whether Liria felt comforted by this she did not say. The last few days leading up to the trip she seemed to be so deep in thought Russell found it difficult to talk with her.

Liria was quiet on the trip to Chicago. Whether it was due to fear or excitement Russell could not tell. Whatever it was, it lifted when she got to the airport. Chicago O'Hare is quite a place. All the newness took over her senses. To Russell the flight was uneventful; to Liria everything was an event. She read the magazine, she watched a movie and said yes to anything the flight attendant offered her.

They change flights in Italy. Her excitement continued. Russell noticed that she was more confident going through security, waiting in line and handling herself in this busy international Airport. Towards the end of the flight to Albania, as they were descending, her face was glued to the window.

"They look so small. The mountains, I mean. From up here, they look so small," she said in a quiet voice.

Russell did not comment but hoped that all her transitions in Albania would also come to appear so small.

Jetlag did not seem to be in Liria's vocabulary. After checking into the guest-house, she went to the market at the corner and bought some fresh fruit. She became instant friends and achieved celebrity status when they found out how long she'd been away from Albania. Shopkeepers slipped an extra apple into her bag or gave her an extra discount. Little old ladies knitting socks by the side of the road insisted she take a pair for free and then caught her up on all the news that never gets in newspapers. And all on her own she went to an ATM machine and withdrew money.

The next day her comments were simple as they drove to her hometown.

"The roads are paved."

"They must've had rain."

"That's a new building."

To all these comments Russell gave a muffled reply. He was trying to let his stomach readjust to the winding and dippy roads of Albania.

When they got to Gurdeti, it seemed as if the entire town was out to greet her. No president, hero or astronaut could have received a warmer welcome. Russell got lost in the crowd trying to keep up. It seemed like it took hours to take a five-minute walk from where they were dropped off to Liria's childhood home. Everyone wanted to get a picture of her with them. Everyone wanted to formally greet her. Even the young people who had never seen her before treated her like a long-lost friend.

Eventually, they got to the house, put the suitcases inside, formal introductions were made and tea served. Liria seemed to be relaxed and in control. She was flipping between English and Albanian with ease. People kept coming with gifts of food and candy. Liria made Russell try everything, always adding the comment, "It's not as good as mine but it's okay."

Russell had planned to spend more time in Gurdeti, but with Liria doing so well, he took an earlier bus back to Tirana.

CHAPTER FOURTEEN

The week went by quickly for Russell. He found he had little time to think about Liria. He was back in his world, and she was back in hers. He did, however, pray for her well-being. Before he knew it he was back on the rickety bus to Gurdeti.

When he pulled into town the Liria that greeted him was not the one from Ferndale. She was not even the same Liria that he dropped off a week ago. She was confident, sure of herself, and appeared to be completely in charge of the entire town.

"Mr. Green, we need to talk," she said in a solemn voice.

Russell was halfway prepared for the shoe to drop. He had been seeing hints of it for some time now.

She sat him down across from her and gently put her hand on his as a mother would in order to comfort a small child. He could tell that she had thought about her words carefully.

"I'm not going back with you. I have decided to stay. This is my home. I feel it in my heart. They need me here. There is so much to do here. I have even started an English class."

Russell kept his face calm but inside he was chuckling.

"And with my money, I can help my sister keep our family's house. But more than just my money, they need to hear my story. Girls are still being married off to prostitution. I am not sure how much I can change here but I need to try."

Russell did not sense that she was going to ask for permission or even his blessing.

"I will miss you," he said honestly.

"You can always come to visit," she said.

"You will have to figure out a way to stay here because you are not from Albania anymore. You're an American citizen." Russell wanted to see how much she had thought this through.

"I talked with our policeman and he said he would help me get the paperwork completed."

They continued talking for over an hour about how she was going to get her money, how much money she could spend a month, where he could mail letters to her, how to do Skype calls, email and all the little details that they could think of.

It was time that he got the bus back to Tirana. They stood up and gave each other a hug. She kissed him gently on the cheek.

"Thank you, Mr. Green. Thank you for everything."

"One more thing," Russell said, hesitating to ask the question that's been on his mind for some time now. "You said that Tody was not the only person buried on the property. Besides your goat William, is there anybody else I should know about?"

"Just the nice man from Romania. He is under the garden shed."

"And just how did he die?"

"He died in his sleep. He wasn't feeling well, he had taken a few aspirin and some sleeping pills. We found him dead in the morning. We buried him the next night and poured a concrete slab over his grave."

When Russell left the house he found out that most of the town was listening in through the windows. Many of them followed him to the bus stop and waved as he got on the rickety bus once again.

On the flight home, the seat next to him was occupied by a marketing executive who wanted to explain to him the new commercials he was designing for a popular breakfast cereal. Russell pretended not to speak much English and drifted off to sleep.

When he got home he found it very quiet. It felt unnatural to have this house all to himself. He occupied his time restocking the refrigerator and making up menu plans. He would have to cook for himself now. He did not know if this made him happy or sad. It took him a few days to gather the courage to go into Liria's room.

What he found there surprised him. She obviously had planned to stay in Albania long before she left. Everything was neat and tidy. There was a box marked "thrift store" and another marked "please store for me". He tried to open the window but it had been painted shut. He wondered how many years she had lived in this room and calculated that that was how old the paint was. Liria was paranoid about drafts, always afraid that a cool breeze would make her sick.

On the way to the grocery store, he stopped in at Charlie's to see how he was doing with his reading lessons. When he pulled into the drive he noticed most of the weeds were gone and there was the beginning of order among the pile of boats. Charlie himself was standing in their midst with a pad of paper and pencil in his hands.

"What's going on Charlie?"

"Well, I decided to practice my reading and picked up a current copy of a boating magazine. I was looking through the ads and found that some people want some parts that I have here. I figure I had better make a list."

They chatted for a while, then Russell headed out to the grocery store.

"Change is coming to Ferndale," he thought to himself.

That Wednesday he found himself making a pot roast for the Chief of Police on his own.

"Well you got rid of Liria, I see. You didn't bury her in the backyard did you?" joked Dave.

"No, she's happily ruling over her little town in Albania. They treat her like royalty. She is even teaching an English class!"

"No way!" laughed Dave. "By the way, this is a good roast. Not as good as Liria's, but it will do."

"How did the trial go with her nephew?"

Dave pushed back his chair, wiped his mouth with a napkin, and said, "Well, thanks to that little book you found they were able to pull together enough evidence to put him away for twenty years. At the last minute, he tried to plea bargain and gave the lawyers names and dates that would send other people to jail. The judge dropped his sentence five years, but I doubt he will survive that. If he does I doubt he would survive long on the outside. The mob does not like people who squeal. And by the way, Liria's name never came up."

"What else did I miss when I was gone?" Russell asked.

"Not much. Giblets came into the restaurant the other day. Said he had been working at the bakery, baking bread, they fired him because he was caught loafing."

"He's an interesting character, what do you know about him?"

"Not much. He doesn't break the law, and as long as he's not doing anything illegal I leave him alone," replied Dave.

"That's the trouble with you, you're only interested in people that break the law."

"Oh? And what laws of you been breaking lately?"

"Me? You just came over for the pot roast," Russell decided not to tell him about the other body under the garden shed. At least not yet.

"Guilty as charged." laughed Dave.

The next day when he went to town, Russell saw Giblet's bicycle outside of Betty's. He went in to meet this strange man.

Giblets was sitting in his usual corner away from everyone else. He quick typed away on an old laptop computer. He was not wearing the face mask that he had on the other day. Russell walked over, held out his hand and introduced himself.

"Hi, I'm Russell Green."

Giblets held up his hands to show that he had on a pair of white cotton gloves.

"Sorry, I'm not shaking hands today, must have gotten into some poison ivy or something," he said. He quickly closed laptop but not before Russell saw what was on the screen. Giblets then sniffled a bit, picked up his things, left some money on the table and walked out, leaving his coffee still untouched.

The waitress came over, sighed, picked up the money and said, "He is always like that, always pays for his coffee but hardly ever drinks it."

Russell walked over to the table of regulars, ordered his own coffee and sat down.

"Don't take it personally, he is like that with everyone; not mean, just unfriendly." said one man.

"Funny with his jokes though." said another.

"He lives out in the woods, in a tin shack."

"Yeah, I saw it, and his phone is on the outside of his house. I asked him why one time and he said that it was because that was where the cable was. Strange man."

"He drives an old army Jeep, probably from back in the '50s or '60s. That Jeep is probably worth more than his whole house if he ever sold it."

"Where did he work today?" Russell asked.

"Oh, it was a good one, he said he thought he had an exciting job as a tailor, but it was only so-so."

"Get it? Sew-sew!" laughed another, making a hand gesture of sewing with a needle and thread.

Russell finished his coffee and got a general idea of where Giblets' house was. Then he went back home. He always believed that everything had a reason. What he figured about Giblets could only point to one problem. He decided to pay him a visit, but first, he had some work to do.

At home, he did a quick internet search of the financial pages. He dug around in his closet for an old pair of white cotton pants he bought back in Istanbul and a white cotton T-shirt. He washed them out in water from the rain barrel outback. While they were drying he took a shower, doing a final rinse with a bucket of rainwater. He was now ready.

He drove his pickup down the dirt road, stopping several yards away from the house. It was as the men had said it was, a completely metal house about sixteen by sixteen feet. There was a front door in the middle of one side with a telephone mounted to the right of it.

Stopping still a few yards off from the house, he called out, "Hey Giblets."

He saw a face briefly at the window. "Go away, I'm busy."

"Or should I say, Gilberto Graft, owner and president of Graft Industries?"

There was a slight pause, then he appeared at the door wearing the face mask. "What else do you know?"

"That you probably have what they call an allergy to the 21st century. So for your safety, I'm wearing all-natural materials, no perfumes or deodorant and I rinsed off in rainwater."

Gilberto took off his mask and smelled the air. "Have a seat," he said, motioning to the edge of the small front porch. "Better stay downwind just in case." He then sat down on the lone wicker chair. "What gave me away?"

"Well, you don't act like the typical homeless bum. You don't associate with anybody, but you're smart. I notice you were looking at the Dow Jones averages on your laptop but you were not touching it with your bare hands. Poison ivy is not in season right now, and besides, you were not scratching. You usually use a bicycle, but when you drive you use one of the most expensive cars in town. You've chosen something void of plastics and electronics. You live in what is basically a Faraday cage. Even your phone is outside."

"Well you got at least one thing wrong, the name is McGraft. It was my marketing team that decided it was too much like McDonald's and made me use just simply 'Graft'."

Russell remained silent, he did not know how much information Gilberto wanted to share.

"About five years ago I started to get ill and the doctors could not figure out what I had. I wasn't going to let them put me on a whole bunch of pharmaceuticals so I did my own research. Some said it was just in my head and recommended a psychiatrist. I did my own experiments and came to the conclusion, as you did, that I was allergic to the 21st century. Plastics, petrochemicals, perfumes, cell phones, radio waves and all the rest."

"Well, you can't run a Fortune 500 company and be allergic to it. So I bought this fifty-acre plot and had a trusted friend build me this house. I sold the company and went into hiding. My secretary still works for me, handling my financial investments. The old army Jeep was a part of my fleet of cars but the only one that I was not allergic to."

"So I am doing okay, living in a small town where people think I am crazy. I make up jokes and use my childhood nickname. I spend my days studying botany, listening to the birds and doing as little business possible. I also have some classic books. My secretary comes by every month or so with papers for me to sign. I order most of my food online but I can handle going into town once in a while. Quite the life of multimillionaire, you think?"

"Well, I am not going to tell," said Russell assuredly. He walked over to the phone and tacked a card up on the wall. "Here is my number if you need anything."

Russell got up to leave and absentmindedly held out his hand.

"I better not risk it, maybe one day," said Giblets.

As he walked back to his pick up truck he called back over his shoulder, "Where did you work today?"

"I had a job changing wheels at the bicycle shop, but it made me too tired."

Russell laugh. "I had a job studying electrons, but it was a negative experience."

"I will keep that one in mind," Giblets said with a smile.

CHAPTER FIFTEEN

Russell was working in the garden, pulling weeds when the black luxury sedan pulled in. Brushing the dirt from his hands he slowly walked over to greet his new guests. They had called the day before asking about particulars of his guesthouse.

The couple in the car was having a discussion so Russell waited until they were finished. The man got out and greeted him.

"So glad you could take us in, we have an early flight to Istanbul tomorrow morning so will be leaving pretty early, around 6:oo am." The man said, getting a suitcase out of the trunk.

"Nice car," commented Russell.

"It's a rental. I ordered a small economy one but this is all they had. They gave it to me for the same price though. Being missionaries we need to save money wherever we can."

Russell noticed that the lady was still sitting in the front seat of the car. The man noticed Russell's glance.

"She is nervous about the flight, she's always like this before we fly back to Turkey. What she needs is a good night of sleep and some peace and quiet."

"Well, nobody's going to bother you here. We are about as quiet as it gets."

"That's why we picked this place. Now if you can show me the room I'll get situated."

Russell showed the man upstairs to the room he had prepared earlier this morning. He then left them alone, mainly because he wanted some time to think. Something was different about these missionaries.

Following a train of thought, he went back upstairs and gently knocked on the door. He heard some whispers and the bathroom door close.

"Come in," said the man.

When Russell walked in, the man was sitting in the chair with his shoes off and his feet up on the bed. Russell must've looked surprised because the man quickly took his feet off the bed.

"Please excuse my casualness, Turkish people are quite laid-back. They usually have footstools, we called them Ottomans, after the Ottoman Empire. What can I do for you?" he said quickly changing the subject.

"There is a dish someone told me how to prepare from somewhere out in the Middle East. It's called something like 'chee kofta'. Have you ever had it?"

"A few times," the man answered hesitantly.

"Well, I have some prepared. I just have to cook it. I came to ask if you like yours fried or baked?"

"Either way is fine with us, but please don't go to any trouble."

"No trouble at all," said Russell.

Russell waited till he was in the kitchen before he called Dave.

"I have a strange question for you, are you looking for anybody?" Russell then gave him a brief description of the man and his reasons for wondering about his real identity.

About an hour later Russell went back upstairs, knocked on the door and once again heard the bathroom door close.

"Come in."

"If you don't mind coming with me downstairs just a minute, I need you to sign my guestbook. I like to keep track of who's coming and going."

"No problem," the man said as he got up and followed Russell to the kitchen.

When he got there he noticed there were three other gentlemen playing cards at the table. A fourth hand had been dealt and was sitting there face down.

"Just our weekly card game," explained Russell, then motioning over to the kitchen counter, he said, "Just sign here."

After he had finished signing, he turned around and noticed the three men were standing up facing him. Two of them had guns drawn and the third had a pair of handcuffs out.

"William Stephenson, you're under arrest for embezzlement and fraud. You have the right to remain silent. Anything you say can and will be used against you in a court of law," Dave said slipping the handcuffs on his wrists. He led him away while finishing the reading of his rights.

One deputy went with them while the other stayed behind.

Slowly they walked back upstairs and knocked on the door.

"Come in," said the lady in a feeble voice.

When they came in they found her sitting on the bed hunched over with tears coming down her face.

"I saw from the window. Am I going to be arrested too?"

"No ma'am, you did nothing illegal, you've only been gullible and if that was a crime we would all be in jail. The officer is here just to pick up Mr. Stevenson's belongings."

"Stevenson?" A look came over her face that was hard to describe. She put her face in her hands in disbelief. "He didn't even tell me his real name."

The officer went about his job quickly and quietly and when he was gone, Russell brought up a sandwich for the lady.

"It's not the Middle Eastern dish I promised you but you probably would not have liked it. You are still free to stay here tonight, but is there anyone you could call to pick you up later? The police took the car, it was stolen."

"I'm not surprised now, how could I have been so stupid?" She paused and took a deep breath. "We met at an office party a month ago."

Russell leaned against the door jam, not wanting to come into her space but still wanting to be there for her, almost as a priest in a confessional.

"It was shortly after my divorce," she went on after a pause, reliving the last few days. "He was exciting to be with, filled with stories of travel and adventure. I guess it woke up a part of me that had been asleep. I felt so alive and wanted. I see I mistook that feeling for love. He said he had made a fortune and that his money was tied up in an offshore bank account. He had a large house on a Caribbean island. We were going to fly there tomorrow. He promised me a life of excitement." she sighed and said, "Well, tonight has definitely been exciting."

Russell turned to leave her alone.

"Wait, how did you figure this out?"

"Well, the first thing was the flight to Istanbul in the morning. There are none; they are all in the evening. Second, that was no rental car. Most rental car companies put their logo on their license plate frames. They also give you a large key tab, neither of which he had. Third, he had the culture wrong, Turkish people generally would not put their feet on the bed, and they certainly would not show the bottom of their feet. And the 'chee kofta' I offered is neither baked nor fried, it's eaten raw, something anybody would know even if they had only been there for a short visit."

"You are quite the detective."

"No ma'am, just a missionary. Goodnight."

"One more thing, he even had me pay for the tickets."

"The police said there was only one ticket, he would have left you at the airport." Russell turned back to face her. "Anyone can hand you an apple, claiming it was from their tree, but give a man time and you will see the fruit he really produces. Next time don't be in such a hurry, you are worth waiting for."

Russell then turned and closed the door.

A little later he heard the lady making a phone call. Sometime just before daybreak a car pulled in and picked her up.

The next morning Russell went into the kitchen and decided to prepare bacon and eggs. While they were frying he made toast and a large pot of coffee. Bacon and eggs were his comfort food. As the aroma of them cooking filled the kitchen, his heart filled with thankfulness and peace.

When breakfast was over and dishes were done he walked to the front porch with his mug of coffee. This is where he usually had his Bible reading, but today he set the Bible aside and decided to go straight to prayer.

"Dear God, this is a funny type of retirement that you've set up for me. Not that I'm complaining. It's just not what I had in mind.

The people and the stories that You've brought into my life are different from anything else I've encountered. I suppose whatever You send my way, You've also prepared me for. So I'm ready for whatever else You send my way in this assignment in Ferndale. Amen!"

AUTHOR BIO

Dan Smeenge has lives on five continents and  several islands. His most interesting house guests have been Kechua Indians, Kosovan refugees, one thousand loose baby chicks, and tarantulas. He is father and grandfather to a wonderfully crazy, totally non-related, multicolored family. He's moved over fifty times, once being a journey down the Mississippi. His first book, "Redeeming River" is also available on Master Releases.